If You Believe

There's only one man she needs to believe in. Him.

When it comes to her love life, the name of Aubrey Mathison's coffee shop says it all: "Bean There, Done That". There's only one harmless man in her life right now—the homeless one parked outside the shop. Except the crazy things he says keep coming true.

She has to laugh at "You'll meet your soul mate today", though. Divorce taught her that men as gorgeous as sexy police chief Price Delacroix are not to be trusted. She's totally up for a one-night stand, but more than that? No, thanks.

Price bears his own scars from the past, but he knows instantly that Aubrey is his. How to convince her he wants more than to be her personal jungle gym? Cut her off. That means no more mattress gymnastics—until she starts seeing things his way.

Aubrey is just as determined Price's campaign to wear down her resistance is going to fail, no matter how wickedly determined he is. Until her resident prophet spouts a new prediction: her soul mate's life is in danger...

Warning: A sexy cop who doesn't take no for an answer, a sassy heroine who knows the power of a good striptease, spankings, anal, and enough variety in hot sexual positions to make your toes curl. Oh, and a slightly crazy guardian angel.

Believe in Me

Love might need a little push...or a good, swift kick.

Tori Chambers. Old biddy, gossip, busybody and meddler. Except in reality she's none of those things—she's a guardian angel who specializes in helping people find their soul mates. Her latest assignment has had her tearing her hair out for over a year. She's holding up her end for the fireman who's her current client, but his soul mate's guardian angel is dropping the ball big time. And when a replacement steps in, it's enough to curl what's left of Tori's hair.

Jericho. The one man who broke her heart—and made her determined to never fail her clients like her own guardian angel failed her.

A hundred years ago, while fighting for Texas independence, Jericho made a mistake that accidentally cost her life. Now that she's forced to make nice and work with him, he's determined not to lose her again. Even if he has to tie her to the bed and make love to her until she's willing to see reason.

Because unknown to Tori, she is his assignment. And if he can't find a way to convince her they're soul mates, they face an eternity of consequences...

Warning: Two humans-turned-angels doing very wicked, non-angelic things to each other. Tied to the bed, bent over the table, up against the wall, and plenty of front and backdoor action is enjoyed by all!

Make Me Believe

She has two words for love. "Make me." Then love changes the rules...

As far as hairstylist Celia Occam is concerned, she's struck out at marriage twice, and there will be no "third time's a charm". So what if one salon employee and the town gossip seem dead set on fixing her up with Prince Charming. She's nobody's princess.

She's all for scratching the occasional itch with the right man, but firefighter Mason Delacroix is all wrong. Besides, with three broken engagements on his romantic rap sheet, even a one-night mattress mambo sounds like a bad idea.

From the first moment Mason encounters Celia's emotional barriers, he's determined to turn up the heat as high as it takes to melt the ice. If the whole town wants to back him up by playing Cupid, he's on board. Track record be damned. He wants Celia, and he's ready for permanent.

When her self-appointed guardian angels conspire to lock them in the basement, their long-denied chemistry explodes. She finds herself relishing every moment—though her subconscious is already on the run.

Funny thing, though. Every time she zigs, Mason's already zagged. Making her wonder if this time it's for real, or if Cupid is just up to its old tricks.

Warning: A hairdresser with a slight fetish for naughty lingerie. A sexy fireman who knows what he wants, which includes having said hairdresser in every possible way. Frontways, backways, sideways...and always.

Look for these titles by
Crystal Jordan

Now Available:

Treasured
Wasteland: The Wanderer

In the Heat of the Night
Total Eclipse of the Heart
Big Girls Don't Die
It's Raining Men
Crazy Little Thing Called Love

✓*Unbelievable*
If You Believe
Believe in Me
Make Me Believe

Forbidden Passions
Stolen Passions
Fleeting Passions

Demon Heat
Demon's Caress

Print Anthologies
Wasteland
Forbidden Passions

Unbelievable

Crystal Jordan

SAMHAIN
PUBLISHING

Samhain Publishing, Ltd.
11821 Mason Montgomery Road, 4B
Cincinnati, OH 45249
www.samhainpublishing.com

Unbelievable
Print ISBN: 978-1-61921-293-0
If You Believe Copyright © 2013 by Crystal Jordan
Believe in Me Copyright © 2013 by Crystal Jordan
Make Me Believe Copyright © 2013 by Crystal Jordan

Editing by Amy Sherwood
Cover by Kanaxa

If You Believe, ISBN 978-1-60504-754-6
First Samhain Publishing, Ltd. electronic publication: September 2009
Believe in Me, ISBN 978-1-60504-894-9
First Samhain Publishing, Ltd. electronic publication: February 2010
Make Me Believe, ISBN 978-1-60928-502-9
First Samhain Publishing, Ltd. electronic publication: July 2011
First Samhain Publishing, Ltd. print publication: June 2013

Contents

If You Believe

Dedication

For Beth, who made me do it.

Chapter One

"The end is near!" the grubby man shouted at Aubrey as she walked past. He waved a big sign that said the same thing in fire engine red letters.

The end of what though? The world? America? Poverty? The bad song blasting out of his boom box? She was hoping for that last one as she dumped some change into the rusted coffee can next to him.

"Hi, Jericho." She gave him a wide berth. The homeless guy was bat-shit crazy, but harmless, and she'd been forking whatever change she had in her pockets into his can for a couple of months. Which she'd done every day since he'd parked his unwashed self on the park bench across from her coffee shop Bean There, Done That.

"Hey, Aubrey!" Jericho gave her a gap-tooth grin before he sobered abruptly, his eyes taking on a weird intensity. "Beware of fire today."

She blinked at him, chills crawling over her skin at the bizarre statement. Opening her mouth to ask what the hell he was babbling about, she stopped. He'd already started humming along with the radio. Yep, the man was certifiable.

"Yeah, okay. Thanks, Jericho." She waved as she jogged across the street through the early morning fog.

A wave of deep satisfaction rolled through her when she approached the front of her shop. It'd been open for over three years and business was booming. She'd moved to Cedarville from Portland after her divorce was final because she needed a change of pace, a change of *place*. She'd caught her ex screwing one of the waitresses at the restaurant they'd owned, so she'd screwed him in the divorce settlement. Was she bitter? Hell, yes. Almost eight years as Mrs. Scott Roberts had gotten her nothing except a broken heart and broken dreams.

Scott had cured her of her girlish longings for love and commitment. Now she kept it light and fun with the men she dated. She'd found it was easier for everyone that way. No one got hurt, especially not her.

Unlocking the side entrance, she turned off the security system and went through the routine of opening up the shop. After the chaos and rush of being the head pastry chef at a *chichi* restaurant in Portland, Bean There, Done That was nirvana. The mornings were her alone time, when the whole world came down to this Zen place with just her, the ovens, and the smell of baking pastries and fresh brewed coffee.

Susan would be in soon to help Aubrey with the morning rush, but this time was all Aubrey's. The time flew by and before she knew it, Susan's massive combat boots were tromping into the kitchen. Glancing up, Aubrey stifled a snort. Over the boots, Susan wore a lacy black Victorian style dress. "Heya, Aubrey."

The only dress code for employees was that they wear a black outfit with the black and green Bean There, Done That apron over it. Susan liked to take the uniform to the next level. "Morning."

The younger woman checked the daily menu Aubrey had written on the chalkboard out front and then took the chairs off the tables to set up for the day. Thirty minutes until they opened. They worked in companionable silence. One of the reasons she had Susan on the morning shift was that she didn't chatter.

Wiping a last bit of flour off her hands, Aubrey turned to Susan before walking into the back room. "I'll grab the last batch of lemon cakes out of the oven if you watch the glaze on the stove."

"Sure thing, boss lady." Susan's braids bobbed when she nodded.

Just as Aubrey flipped off the ovens and pulled out the hot pans a shriek came from the front. Her heart seized in terror before it leaped into a gallop. Slapping the pans onto the cooling racks, she raced for the other room. Flames danced across the stovetop, and Susan lay in a crumpled heap on the floor. "Susan!"

A customer wandered in the door, and Aubrey rounded on him like a madwoman. "Do you have a cell phone?"

He nodded, staring blankly from her to the fire. "Then go outside *and call 911.*"

Reality seemed to hit him. He jerked his cell out of his pocket, spun and bolted for the door. She turned back to Susan.

"Oh. God." *OhGodOhGodOhGod.* Sweat ran in rivulets down Aubrey's face, her heart pounding so hard she thought it might explode.

The fire hit a dishtowel that had flopped onto the floor near Susan. No time to grab the fire extinguisher. Dropping to her hands and knees, Aubrey crawled as fast as she could to Susan's side, wrapped an arm around her and slid her as far away from the flames as possible. The heat rolled over Aubrey, drying her eyes out while every instinct inside her screamed to *run.* To escape the danger. But she couldn't leave the younger woman.

Aubrey hacked and wheezed as the smoke got thicker. Jesus, she needed to get the fire extinguisher. Staggering to her feet, she snatched the bright red canister off the wall. The smoke seemed to follow her, and when she spun she realized that the ends of her hair were on fire. Terror exploded through her and she frantically slapped the flames out, her shriek dissolving into a whistling cough as the smoke burned her throat. A sob bubbled up, but she ripped the pin out of the extinguisher and hosed the stove down with white foam. It went everywhere, all over the stove, her, the counters, her, the floor, her. Smoke boiled up while the flames slowly died out.

Whooping sounded in the air as the whole fire department, an ambulance and a police car rolled up to the front of the shop. Thank God. Tears streamed from her eyes, as much from relief and residual fear as from the acrid smoke. Her lungs burned like she'd sucked the flames down her throat. She sank to her knees beside Susan and closed her eyes. No way was she leaving Susan alone in here, even if the fire was out.

The firefighters bundled both women up and got them out, slapping an oxygen mask on Aubrey in the process. Smoke inhalation, they said. Yeah, she could believe it. She grabbed one fireman's sleeve. Fire damage and the mask made her sound like Darth Vader. "Will she be okay?"

Mason Delacroix. She knew this man. He ordered a black coffee every day at noon. He nodded down at her. "Yeah. She seems to be doing all right. Looks like she's waking up. We'll know more when they get her to Cedarville General."

Aubrey clamored into the ambulance beside Susan, ignoring the protest from one of the paramedics. What was he going to do, toss her out? They both knew she was going to have to get checked out by a doctor anyway. This way it was one trip for Susan *and* Aubrey.

Only then did it occur to her that her business was trashed. Shit on a stick. A million details bounced through her head, but she couldn't focus on one of them. Police reports, insurance claims, cleaning up the mess. God, what a mess. It was too much for her right now. Her thoughts slid away, so she closed her eyes and let herself rest. Just for a moment. Weariness dragged at her very bones, and she hung on to

Susan's hand as the ambulance sped through the normally quiet streets of her little town.

"How's that?" Celia Occam, Aubrey's flamboyant best friend *cum* hairstylist, spun the chair around so she could look at herself. Today Celia wore ragged blue jeans and ropes of black pearls. Somehow she pulled it off. With style.

She'd cut the scorched ends off Aubrey's long hair. Instead of the waist length, flat mahogany sheet she usually wore, Celia had layered it up to Aubrey's bra strap and thrown some highlights in. It made her look younger than thirty-four and set off the grey-blue of her eyes. She turned her head to get a peek at the back. "Nice. Very nice."

"I know." Twirling the silver cape away from Aubrey's shoulders, Celia brushed a few stray hairs off her customary black shirt.

"Yeah, you've just been waiting for an excuse to do whatever you want to my hair." Aubrey's voice came out a smoky drawl. Her throat still ached a bit from the smoke, but the doctor said she would be fine in no time.

"Hell, yes, girlfriend." Celia smirked, and Aubrey rolled her eyes in return.

The bell over the door tinkled, and both Celia and Aubrey turned towards it to see who was coming in. Celia groaned and closed her eyes before offering the newcomer a glare. Aubrey bit her lip to hide a grin that might get her scalped bald. Mason Delacroix was the bane of Celia's existence. He asked her out at least once a week. Aubrey had no idea why her friend kept turning him down. He was a firefighter, built like a Greek god, and had a Vin Diesel thing going on with his shaved head. If that wasn't enough, his green eyes always had a twinkle of wicked mischief in them. The man was beyond good looking. Hell, if he wasn't so into her best friend, *she'd* ask him out

19

herself.

Celia claimed that she didn't want to settle down and that he was the marrying kind, but Aubrey just thought that meant she was being a pansy about it. She didn't have to let it go far enough to be serious. Shag him and get it out of her system was Aubrey's advice. Celia hadn't taken the suggestion so far.

He arched a brow and grinned at Celia. "Don't worry. I'm not here for you...this time."

Her brown eyes narrowed to slits, and Aubrey thought she saw the barest flash of jealousy on the hairstylist's face. "Who are you here for then? And why couldn't it wait until *after* she left my salon?"

"Seeing you is the bonus, honey. I need to speak to Ms. Mathison."

Pursing her lips at him, Aubrey lifted her eyebrows. "Oh, do not put me in the middle of the little hard-to-get games you two play."

But his face fell into serious lines. "I've gone over every inch of your shop with the Fire Marshall, and we have questions about why the alarm and sprinkler system didn't go off because your building and system are up to fire code."

"Oh." She blinked, processing the abrupt change of topic. She'd been so focused on getting out of the fire that she hadn't even thought about the sprinkler system—and now she felt completely stupid for *not* thinking about it. "Shit. That was an expensive system too. What the hell happened?"

"We think it was a malfunction. Nothing looked tampered with." He nodded, total confidence radiating from his handsome face, and she finally got why everyone assumed he was a shoo-in to take over the fire department in the next few years. "However, Price wants to meet with you personally to take your report and go over the events of yesterday."

Price Delacroix was the new Chief of Police and Mason's

older brother. He'd followed Mason to Cedarville a few months before. She hadn't met him yet, but the buzz around town was that he was a hotshot ex-SWAT officer from L.A. and that he was as gorgeous as his brother. Not that she gave a flying rat's ass what he looked like right now. She needed to get her livelihood back up and running. A malfunctioning fire system was a glitch she did not need—not to mention how that piece of news was going to go over with her insurance company.

A headache began to throb, and she rubbed a hand over her forehead. "All right then. You'll be in touch about this later, won't you?"

"Count on it." His broad shoulder lifted in a shrug. "I'm sorry about all of this, Aubrey."

"Thanks." She sighed, shrugging to stretch the tight muscles in her neck and arms. At least Susan was okay—her mother would pick her up and take her home later that day. All she'd had was a mild concussion after she'd tripped over her combat boots and cracked her head on the counter, spilling glaze all over the stove and starting the fire.

Bean There, Done That wasn't quite as lucky as the two of them. The police had taped off Aubrey's shop until an officer could come take her statement. She was meeting him in half an hour. Apparently, that meant she was meeting with the chief himself. She winced. A part of her did *not* want to see the mess she knew would be inside. It had looked bad enough from the *outside* this morning. Her shop was the refuge she'd used to get over the heartache of her divorce. Seeing it damaged and broken was not something she relished, especially with this extra complication Mason just threw in her lap.

"Okay, honey. I need to go take care of this. Thank you, you're a genius and my personal hair goddess." She smacked a kiss on Celia's cheek and handed her enough bills to pay for the new hairdo and a big tip.

Grinning, Celia gave her a quick hug. "Take care, honey."

21

Crystal Jordan

"Thanks." Aubrey tugged her purse strap over her shoulder and walked outside. Celia's salon, Occam's Razor, was on the opposite side of the park that made up the town square.

Aubrey jogged across the street, already fishing in her pocket for some change for Jericho. She couldn't see him through the trees yet, but he was always there. He was as reliable as rain in the Pacific Northwest. And there he was, his scraggly hat coming into view. His boom box blasted out old '70s rock today—a major improvement over yesterday's ear grinding noise. He smiled when he spotted her. "Hey, Aubrey! Sorry about your shop."

Sudden tears smarted her eyes, and she had to stare up at the sky for a minute to keep them from falling. How bad would it be in there? She swallowed and dropped the coins into his coffee can. "Mornin', Jericho."

"Are you all right?" Concern swam in his grey eyes, and he snatched off his hat to crumple it between his filthy hands. His hair stood up in ragged silver patches. "I didn't mean to make you cry."

"Don't worry about it." She folded her arms over her T-shirt and sniffled.

He laced his fingers together over his flat belly. "Well, I believe everything happens for a reason. There's a logic to this happening."

Her mouth dropped open, and for probably the first time in her life, she had no idea what to say. She sputtered for a long moment, just staring at the crazy man. "Who's logic are we talking about?"

"The Man Upstairs of course."

Shaking her head, she continued to stare as if he'd grown a second head. "You amaze me, Jericho. You're sitting there on a park bench—homeless—and you're talking about how everything is right with the world."

"What do you believe in, Aubrey?" His silver gaze sharpened as he focused on her face. She felt pinned in place, a bug in a high school science lab.

Narrowing her eyes, she refused to feel uncomfortable. His religion was not her issue—and she didn't have to agree with him. Besides, how many people got *everything is sunshiny because of God* speeches from hobos? It was unreal. She was having one hell of a weird couple of days. "Are you trying to convert me, Jericho?"

He chuckled. "I asked what *you* believe in. I don't need to covert anyone. My faith is what it is."

"Okay. Fine." She jammed her fists down on her hips. "What's the reason my shop caught fire?"

"That's easy." A contented smile washed over his face and the intense moment was gone. He whistled a little tune. His voice was just this side of dreamy when he said, "So you could meet your soul mate today."

She rolled her eyes and spun away. Why was she debating with a nut ball? She was going to have to start questioning her own sanity. *Soul mate? Riiiiight.* She didn't believe in soul mates. She'd given up on love a long time ago. Been there, done that. She'd named her shop that for a reason. It was her motto. Scott was the only man she'd ever imagined coming close to being a *soul mate.* And he'd made sure she didn't have any illusions left after the divorce about how much she had lacked as a wife and life partner. Love? Soul mates? She snorted.

A big, muscular man leaned against the side of a Crown Victoria outside her shop. His gaze followed her as she left Jericho and walked over to meet him. That had to be Chief Delacroix. He looked too much like Mason to be anyone else. In a town as small as Cedarville, she could identify everyone who lived here on sight. And this man had never been in her coffee shop. A shame too. He certainly was pretty to look at—even better looking than Mason, and that was saying something.

23

He looked her over, assessing her. Something sparked in his green gaze but was masked in a professional demeanor before she could decide what it was. "Mrs. Mathison?"

"It's Ms. and call me Aubrey." She offered her hand for him to shake.

"Price Delacroix." He had a world-weary cynicism in his eyes that made her look twice. Everything about the man made her come back for a second helping. Emerald eyes, tanned skin, close-cropped dark hair, muscles that rippled under his shirt and slacks. Yum.

When his big hand engulfed hers, a shiver of pure sex went down her spine. Oh baby. She swallowed and tried to come up with something intelligent to say. "The new police chief. From L.A."

"Yes, ma'am." She winced at the *ma'am*. Jesus, she wasn't that old. Thirty-four was *not* old damn it.

He jerked his chin towards the coffee shop, indicating that she should precede him. She fished around for her keys and headed for the side door. The heat from his big body embraced her, and she felt crowded up against the door. Her hormones made it clear they wouldn't mind a bit more crowding. She cleared her throat. "So what brings you to Cedarville?"

The first thing that hit her when she opened the door was the stench. Acrid. Smothering. Disgusting. Her business always smelled of coffee and baked goods. Now it made her stomach turn. She swallowed the lump in her throat.

"I wanted a change of pace." His gaze swept the big room where she kept most of the industrial size ovens and cooling racks. An enormous stainless steel prep table dominated the middle of the room. Through a swinging door opposite of the side entrance was the main room where the fire had happened. Even from here she could see damage. Smoke and soot had stained the ceiling. Black dust covered everything. The swinging door was twisted and warped from heat.

"Burn out, huh?" She grabbed on to the conversation with the police chief for dear life. Anything to keep from thinking about how long this was going to close her shop for repairs. She turned her back on the damage and faced him. A lot of city people moved to Cedarville to get away from the high pressure of city life. She should know—she was one of them.

"Something like that." That cynical gaze swept down her body, and she saw what kind of assessment he was doing. Sexual, carnal.

Heat followed in the wake of his gaze. Her fingers tightened into fists, what was wrong with her? Her livelihood was trashed and she was getting wet over some guy she'd just met. Then again, if her business was in shambles, wringing herself out with a pretty man was a nice distraction. A slow smile curled her lips, and she gave him a very thorough and obvious once-over. "Married?"

"I was once. I'm divorced. You?" He crossed his arms over his chest, and she could see the delineation of his big muscles through his dress shirt.

She shook her head. "Same. Kids?"

"Nope."

"Me neither." *So you could meet your soul mate today.* Jericho's words came back to her in a quick rush, but she pushed the thought away. Soul mate? Yeah, right. Bedmate? *We might have a winner here.* She grinned.

He arched a brow, but smiled back. Man, he had a killer smile. A flash of white teeth and the sexiest dimples she'd ever seen. His expression said he knew exactly what she was thinking, and he more than reciprocated, but his voice was all business. He pulled a pad of paper and pen out of his suit jacket. "I'm here to take your statement. About the fire."

She nodded and forced herself to face the destruction. It

25

was just as bad as it had been, and she swayed a little on her feet as the details bombarded her again. Strong arms caught her, tugged her against a broad chest. She leaned against him, buried her nose in his chest and inhaled the scent of *him* and his spicy cologne, and let herself be weak for a moment longer. But the feel of his hard planes molding to her softer curves sent a shock of lust through her that curled her toes. One of his hands stroked up her spine and bracketed the nape of her neck, tilting her head back until she looked him in the eyes. They really were the most incredible shade of green. Her body reacted, loosening some muscles, tightening others as it prepared for sex. She could feel the impressive length of his erection riding against her belly. Moisture flooded her core, and her pussy clenched. Her nipples hardened while the rest of her melted against him, a throb of utter want going through her. His gaze sharpened, focusing on her lips and she was certain he was going to kiss her. The heat reflected in his eyes was enough to burn.

Burn.

The word jolted her back to reality. She was standing in her burned-out building ready to shove a man she'd only just met against the nearest wall and jump his bones. What the hell was the matter with her?

"Are you all right, Ms. Mathison?" His voice was a harsh rasp, showing that he was as affected by this as she was. It was a very small comfort. His grip on her eased, and her hormones whimpered at the loss of contact. His tone gentled. "Aubrey?"

Forcing herself to pull away, she shoved a hand through her newly shortened hair and waved the other in a vague circle that encompassed the room. "I—I'm fine. Sorry about that. It's shocking seeing it like this."

"It's hard to see something you love in shambles." He squeezed her shoulder gently before stepping away. "Are you ready?"

She swallowed and nodded. Somehow it was bearable with him there as a solid, steady presence. It emanated from the man—rock-solid, dependable, a man who'd seen it all and still held people's hands when their lives fell apart. Like he had with her. It was odd to *know* so much about him in just those few moments of interaction, but somehow she was certain she wasn't wrong. She could understand why they'd hired him as police chief.

Working their way through the shop, she explained the details of what happened the day before. What she could remember of it. Some of it was a confused blur of chaos, heat and panic. She doubted she'd ever remember all of what happened clearly. Her throat was parched and swollen from all the talking when she came to a halt beside the stove. "So, are we done here?"

"Yes." He tucked his pen and paper back in his jacket. "You can pick up the report this afternoon."

"Thanks." Then she'd have make sure it got to her insurance agency, schedule some estimates for repairs, close down until the repairs were complete and they got the horrible stink out of her shop. A headache throbbed behind her eyes when she started making a list of everything she had to do, and she shoved all thought of the delicious Chief Delacroix from her mind. She had bigger things to deal with.

If Jericho was right, and the Big Man Upstairs did this on purpose, she was ready to kick Him in the shins for it.

Chapter Two

A week later, she was checking the progress on Bean There, Done That. Her insurance agent was still duking it out with the company that had installed the sprinkler system, but she'd gotten the green light on starting repairs. She had a feeling Price had stepped in and smoothed over a few bumps for her in that little snafu. He'd never said anything about it, but he'd been by a few times to see how she was doing, always polite, always watchful, always with that shimmer of too-tempting awareness in his gaze.

Shoving her hands in her pockets, she ignored thoughts of Price and focused on her shop. The nauseating smell seemed to have dissipated. Thank goodness. The ceiling and floor tiles around the stove needed replacing, as did the stove and the counter beside it. A fresh coat of paint would cover up the blackened wall behind the stove. Every bit of cloth, from curtains to chair cushions to dishrags had to go. They all stank of smoke.

She'd already hired a crew who specialized in fire damage to scrub the place from top to bottom and had done a whole lot of the nasty work herself. Bone-deep exhaustion sapped at her strength, but Bean There, Done That was starting to look as good as ever. A little spark of joy lit inside her. She rubbed her hand down the new door that separated the front and back rooms.

Yeah. Everything was going to be okay. Some quiet panic that had gripped her belly and weighed on her chest since she'd seen the damage began to ease. Bean There, Done That had been her lifeline, her escape. A shaky sigh eased past her lips.

After all the workmen filed out for the day, she locked up behind them and walked across the street. She had to pass through the park to get home. Jericho sat in his normal place on the park bench. Her stride checked a bit when she saw him. His prediction about the fire still freaked her out a bit.

Get over yourself, Aubrey. The man is off his meds. She snorted and jogged across the street, automatically rooting around the bottom of her purse for coins. Crazy or not, he was a vagabond with no real way to get food.

He smiled his usual smile as she approached. "Hi there. How's the restoration coming?"

"Just peachy, thanks." She handed over the change. "How're you?"

"Good, good." He waved her off. She sped past, relieved he didn't say anything weird this time. A ridiculous amount of gratitude filled her at the reprieve. "Hang on a second, Aubrey."

Freezing, she muttered every curse she knew under her breath. She even came up with a couple of inventive compound cusswords. Smiling—and hoping it didn't look more like a grimace—she turned around. "Yeah?"

Mr. Crazy Man was back. He hummed a little before speaking again. "Dogs are bad luck for you today."

Shit. She hunched her shoulder and spun away. "Thanks."

If she went her normal route home, she'd have to pass by the dog park that made up a corner of the town square. Maybe she would try a different way. Just for the change of scenery. Change was good for the soul, wasn't it? If she went by the dog park, it just seemed like too much self-fulfilling prophecy.

Taking a left off the main path where she usually took a right, she wandered into the older district of town that had great Victorian houses. She'd always loved that style of architecture, but Scott had wanted modern. Now that she lived alone, it just seemed like too much upkeep. And maybe it was

29

because she was afraid it would put her one step away from crazy cat lady to rattle around in a big old house like that. She turned the corner on to her street. She had four blocks left to go.

"Woof." Her blood ran cold at the deep bark that came from behind her. A lot of people walked these streets in the evening. And took their dogs with them.

A kid of about twelve had lost the leash on his Great Dane. The air went whistling out of her in what might have been a high-pitched squeak.

It wasn't that she believed Jericho or anything, but the fire thing had kind of creeped her out. Watching that pony-sized excuse for a dog running at her made her blood run cold. Anyone would freak out. It had nothing to do with Jericho's warning. Nope. Not a thing.

She backpedaled as fast as her legs could carry her just the same. The back of her ankles hit something that yelped and the next thing she knew she was going down hard on the pavement. Her back arched when her tailbone made sharp contact with the ground and all the breath rushed out of her lungs. Curling into a fetal position on her side, she wrapped her arms around her knees and tried remember why she didn't want to die right then.

When she opened her eyes, a pointy little muzzle snapped in her face as a dachshund yapped. Dog breath, *blech.* She groaned and pushed into a sitting position. A strong arm wrapped around her back to cradle her against a wide chest. *Price Delacroix.*

"Don't move, Aubrey." His deep voice rumbled, and that was all it took to get her hot and bothered. Her sex dampened at the sound of his rich, deep tones. The way he smelled. The hardness of his muscles against her body. *Thank you, Jesus.*

"I'm fine." She tried to pretend the breathiness of her voice was just from having the wind knocked out of her. The way her nipples tightened and her muscles softened told her it was a lie.

"You took a hard fall. Stay there." His words were almost harsh, but his touch was gentle when he brushed her hair away from her face. She fought the urge to lean her cheek into his palm. Everything about this man made her react.

Her original assessment that the two of them were destined to burn up the sheets was dead on. She really wanted to try him on for size. She'd bet he fit just fine. "I'm really all right, Chief."

"Price. You'll call me Price." His other arm slid under her bent knees and lifted her as he stood.

She squeaked and clutched his shoulders. His soft T-shirt bunched in her fingers as she held on tight. "Don't drop me."

A wicked grin flashed over his face before he focused on her eyes. Some of her panic must have shown because he cuddled her closer. "Not a chance, sugar."

"Is she all right, Chief Delacroix?" Mrs. Chambers, the biggest gossip in town, reined in her wiener dog and stared at the two of them.

"Oh, she's fine. Ma'am." He dipped his head in a nod, dismissing the older woman while he turned to walk up the driveway in front the big Victorian on the corner. She sighed in envy when she saw it.

She glanced over his shoulder at Mrs. Chambers. An avid gleam entered the older woman's eyes as he mounted the porch. Pitching her voice low, Aubrey had to warn him. "Look, I know you're new in town, but Mrs. Chambers—"

He nudged the front door of his house open, and then kicked it shut behind them. "Will spread it all over town that I carried you into my house? And will probably embellish it by saying that I practically stripped you on the sidewalk and fucked you against the street lamp."

"She won't say 'fuck', but yeah." She arched her eyebrows. If people wanted anything to be discreet in a small town, they made damn sure the town gossip did not find out. He was from L.A. Maybe he thought it was only in Mayberry TV-land that gossips told the whole town, who then knew your business, and felt free to chat with you about it.

"Well, that's fine." He sounded unruffled as he set her on his kitchen counter. Oh, man. The whole place looked like something out of *Architectural Digest*. She almost whimpered.

Focus, Aubrey. Future sex life at stake here. She was not interested in having her customers comment about her boffing the police chief. Even if she intended to do so. "Um, you know I have to live in this town? And no nice girl is going to date you now because they'll think we're an item. It doesn't matter if they all know Mrs. Chambers is making it up."

"Then we'll have to make it the truth. You'll just have to date me." He shrugged and started to feel her up. She told herself he was just checking for injuries, but her hormones didn't care. Price was here, and he was sliding those big, strong hands over her body.

She clenched her teeth to hold back a different kind of whimper. "And fuck you against a street lamp? I think not."

"We can improvise." He angled a cocky glance up at her. "Fucking me in my house is close enough."

She laughed, inserting as much derision in her tone as possible. He didn't need to know that the thought of fucking him anytime, anywhere, made her quiver, did he? No. No, he didn't. And that was her final answer...at least until they'd gone out once or twice. Well, once would probably do at this point.

She pushed herself forward on the counter until her feet touched the floor. "Well, thanks so much for—"

His eyebrow arched, and that wicked flash of white teeth in his tanned face was her only warning before he crowded her against his cupboard. His hands braced on either side of her. Trapped. He leaned forward until his eyes were level with hers, until his lips were a whisper away from her mouth. "Laugh now, sugar. But I'll have you stripped bare and in my bed tonight. Count on it."

She swallowed hard, fumbling for something witty to say, but nothing came to mind. Heat spiraled tight within her belly, and liquid flooded her pussy.

"I—" Her breath rushed out on a whoosh as she pictured them together, naked on soft sheets in a big bed. *Oh. God. Yes.* She wanted that so much. Her heart leapt and began to race, the muscles in her legs shaking with the effort to keep her upright.

The sides of his eyes crinkled when he grinned. His green gaze dropped to her lips, and they tingled. She licked them, and his gaze followed the motion. One hand lifted to bracket her jaw and hold her in place while he closed the infinitesimal distance between them to brush his mouth over hers.

She shouldn't let him get away with his cocky proclamation about sexing her up, but damn. The man could kiss. Her mind went hazy, and time seemed to stretch. His lips played over hers in slow, worshipful sweeps. Not demanding, not taking. It wasn't what she'd expected. Nothing about him was what she expected. She shouldn't let him touch her, but right now she couldn't remember why.

His hands curved around her ribs, one sliding down to cup her backside, the other moved up to palm her breast. He pulled her pelvis flush against his, and the ridge of his cock rubbed her through their pants. She wanted him inside her. She burned with the craving. Still he kissed her, licking his way into her mouth, twining his tongue with hers. His thumb chafed her nipple, circling the nub until lightning strikes of pleasure flashed from her breast to her pussy. A moan tore from her throat and she tried to climb him, wrapping her legs around his waist.

A low groan rumbled in his chest as he ground against her. She fisted her fingers in his hair, sucked his lower lip into her mouth and arched into him.

Ripping his mouth from hers, he let his head drop back. She slid her tongue up his throat, the hot, masculine taste of his flesh flooding her mouth. His breath hissed between his teeth. "Aubrey—"

"Price." She bit the corded muscle in his neck and he shuddered, jerked back and set her on her feet. Swaying, she slid her hands over the muscled planes of his chest.

"So, I was just about to have dinner." He grabbed her wrists, stilling her movements. Her breath caught and her eyes popped wide in shock as he stepped away from her. The shrill beep of a timer going off echoed in the big kitchen. He smiled. "Right on time."

"You're *stopping*?" She was going to kill him. Dead. Her whole body screamed with want, her skin felt too tight, and she would implode any moment.

He stroked a finger down her arm, and goose bumps followed in the wake of his touch. "You've never heard of foreplay, sugar?"

Shoving both hands in her hair, she tried to straighten the mess. "That was more than foreplay, damn it."

"Not the way I do it."

Damn him, now she wanted to know how he did it. She bit back a snarl. She had two options here. She could stomp out in a huff for him toying with her and leaving her high and dry. Wet. Whatever. Or, she could eat dinner and then make him carry through on all those promises. The needs rushing through her body made the first one a non-option.

"Okay. We'll do it your way." She grabbed the edge of her T-shirt and pulled it over her head, dropping it on the counter.

Her bra was a barely-there scrap of lace, and the cool air brushing over her arms and midriff made her shiver.

His eyes heated as he took in her bare skin, but wariness also flashed in his gaze. "What are you doing?"

She offered him up a smile sweet enough to send him into sugar shock. "Foreplay."

His breath whooshed out as she flicked open the snap on her jeans and made a slow show of pushing them down her legs. He reached for her when she stepped out of the denim. She danced out of his reach, smacking his hands away. "Ah, ah, ah. What's for dinner? I'm *starving*."

"You little—"

Arching an eyebrow, she ran her fingertip around the lace band of her panties. "Don't start a game you don't want to play, Chief."

"Oh, I want to play," he growled, emerald fire flickering in his eyes.

"Good." She sauntered over to the stove to peek in and see what they were having. Some kind of casserole. It smelled great. She didn't care, she just wanted Price to touch her again, but she'd play this out to the end.

Eating was a dance of erotic pleasure. Every movement, every bite, every breath heightened the need between them until she could have cut through the sexual tension in the room with a knife. Her nipples were so hard the lace of her bra brushing against them was painful. Her underwear was damp with moisture, and she kept her thighs crossed tightly to try and suppress some of the ache between them. A hot blade of want sliced through her until she couldn't stand it anymore. Setting her plate aside, she stood from the dinner table.

In one fluid motion, he was on his feet, blocking her path. "Going somewhere, sugar?"

"Yes."

35

He folded his arms across his broad, muscled chest. "Oh?"

Giving him the kind of smile that should have sent his blood rushing straight to his groin, she spun toward the staircase. She let her fingers trail up the silky smooth wood of the banister as she mounted the steps. His heavy tread followed her up. Her breathing sped until she was almost panting with the excitement twisting deep within her. Reaching behind her, she unsnapped her bra and tugged it off to hang on the newel post at the top of the stairs. The wide balcony overlooked the living room as well as the dining room with their abandoned dishes.

An open doorway directly across from her showed rumpled navy blue sheets on a king size bed. Grinning, she spun around and crossed an arm over her breasts to cover herself from his view.

He chuckled. "You can't play shy now, sugar."

For each step he took forward, she took one back. He jerked his T-shirt over his head and dropped it on the carpet. The backs of her knees hit the mattress and she let herself fall. She cupped her hands around her breasts, tweaking the nipples with her fingers. He groaned. Slipping one hand down over the swell of her stomach, she dipped into the damp lace of her panties. "You seem to think I have a problem starting without you."

"Oh Jesus." He stripped out of his jeans so fast, she wouldn't have been surprised if he had rug burns on his legs. Which was fine with her—he deserved some pain for making her stop for dinner earlier.

He didn't wear underwear. Interesting. A smile curved her lips as she looked him over in all his sculpted glory. He was beyond beautiful. Golden skin stretched taut over hard muscles. His cock jutted in a heavy upward arc. The fading sunlight from the window flashed on the bead of moisture at the tip of his dick.

She bit her lip and rubbed her fingertips over her clit. Her knees fell open against the mattress, and she arched into her hand. Moisture slicked her fingers as she circled her clit slowly, teasing herself, teasing him. His brilliant green gaze burned a path from her taut nipples to her lace-covered pussy. She could feel the way he moved his gaze over her like a caress, and it only made her yearning deeper. Choking on a breath, she plunged two digits into her hot channel, fucking herself with her fingers while he watched. "Now, Price. I want you *now.*"

"You don't have to tell me twice." Kneeling on the bed, he reached for her and froze. Then he stood and turned away.

She propped herself on one elbow, her fingers stilling as uncertainty darted through her. "Price?"

He flipped on the light in his bathroom and rifled for something in his medicine cabinet. When he came back, he lifted his palm to show her a handful of silver condom packages. He tossed them on the nightstand.

Oh. Embarrassment curled through her. She hadn't even thought of protection. She always practiced safe sex, and she was so out of her head for this guy...she hadn't considered something as basic as condoms. Her lips twisted. This was not good. In fact, it was dangerous and stupid. What the hell was she doing messing with someone like Price? He had the tall, dark, and cynical thing that she found incredibly attractive, even likeable. He was the kind of man who was easy to fall for, and she wasn't interested in falling. The kind of man she avoided, the chemistry too potent to control, too dark, too complicated.

She shuddered and refocused on him when his fingers curved around her knee. Instant reaction, her body flashing hot as tingles exploding over her skin. His other hand lifted her palm to his lips. "Something wrong, sugar?"

His heavy-lidded gaze watched for her response, assessing her. But desire underlay the penetrating look. He wanted her—

37

she could see how much. Answering need throbbed through her, reminding her why she had agreed to this in the first place. Could she do this just once and not get addicted?

His lips played over the sensitive flesh of her palm, biting the base of her thumb. The slight pain was nothing to the dart of pleasure that went through her. She closed her eyes and swallowed. Fire skated over her flesh in rolling waves. She wanted this too much. She couldn't turn away from it. From him.

Just this once.

"No, nothing worth mentioning." She grinned at him, holding his gaze as she reached for his cock. Every muscle in his big body tensed as she stroked up and down the long length of him. She massaged the glistening beads of cum that dripped from the head of his dick into his hot flesh. His veins pulsed beneath the skin, his cock jerking in her hand.

His breath hissed out when she rolled her palm over the head of his dick and used the other to cup the heavy sac at the base of his thick shaft. "Aubrey."

"Kiss me."

He chuckled, swooping down to cover her mouth with his. There was no gentleness now, no slow seduction. Just hot, naked want. His hands cupped her breasts, pushing them together so he could suck each of the nipples into his mouth. When he bit down on one tight crest, she slid her fingers in his hair and tugged on the silky strands. Her body bowed and writhed underneath him as he batted her nipple with his tongue, shoving it against the roof of his mouth.

"Condom," she gasped.

Lunging, he swiped a foil packet off the bedside table. A light tremble shook his fingers as he unwrapped the condom and rolled it down the long, hard length of his cock. She loved that she could push him to the edge of his control—she doubted much could make the man's hands shake. It turned her on even more that she could do that to him. Then he hooked his fingers in the waistband of her panties and dragged them down her legs, leaving her nude. She opened her arms as he moved between her thighs.

She arched as he seated himself to the hilt in one swift plunge, wrapping her legs around his flanks. Her pussy fisted around his cock, the stretch almost painful, but even the pain was edged in ecstasy. She bit down on his shoulder hard, the taste of his sweat-damped flesh bursting over her tongue. He shuddered and fucked her hard, his rhythm deep and relentless. She was right there with him, raking her nails down his back, silently demanding everything he had and then some. She wanted *more* and deliberately clenched her inner walls on his cock.

"Jesus, *Aubrey*." He groaned, the sound as helpless and needy as she felt. He ground his pelvis against her, every thrust hitting her just right until she was sobbing for breath. His hot scent filled her nose, as well as the musky smell of sex and sweat. Their flesh slapped together with ruthless strokes, the carnal sound echoing in the room. She was so hot, she thought she'd burst into flames at any moment. And she didn't care. She grabbed the taut globes of his ass, urging him on with soft gasps and cries.

Reaching between them, he rolled his fingertip over her clit, still hammering his cock deep inside her pussy. It was too much. It was exactly what she craved. "Price, Price, *Price!*"

Her sex milked his dick in never-ending waves that dragged her beyond any understanding of pleasure she'd ever had before. Tingles raced over her skin as he continued to penetrate her, driving her orgasm to new depths until every muscle in his big body locked and he came too. Another spasm shook her and made her sob, a single tear sliding down her cheek.

God, nothing had ever felt so perfect in her entire life. It was crazy. He groaned and sank on top of her. She held him close, allowing herself a single moment to breathe in his scent and feel the solid heat of his body against hers. It was comforting and warm contentment wound through her. She sighed. Her eyes drifted shut, and she stroked a hand down his back. She'd get herself together and go in a few minutes.

She was asleep before she finished the thought.

Chapter Three

Sunshine filtered through her eyelids. God, it was morning already? She rolled on to her back and stretched her arms over her head, arching her back. When she opened her eyes, she realized that she wasn't in her own bedroom. These weren't her sheets or pillows. When she took a deep breath, the mellow spiciness of Price's cologne came to her. Glancing over, she saw that he wasn't in bed with her. She could hear the shower running in his bathroom.

She grinned and stretched, her muscles pleasantly sore. *Mmm-hmm.* The best sex of her life. With a very creative and naughty man. Images from the night before flipped through her mind. She'd lost count of the number of times he'd made her come. That same sweet contentment flooded her, and the smile widened on her lips. Then she stopped herself, every muscle going rigid. There was no *contentment* allowed with a man—that led to dangerous things. Like thinking she was in love. Believing he loved her back. Relationships. Entanglements. Complicated shit she'd written off when she signed her divorce papers.

Panic exploded in her belly. Time to get the hell out of here. Throwing her legs over the edge of the bed, she stood. Where were her clothes? Oh, yeah. Downstairs. Picking up the sheet they'd kicked off the bed, she tucked it around herself and tiptoed for the door. If she could get out of here before he got out of the shower, she'd be home free. Yes, it was gutless and cowardly, but she needed *out of here*. She needed to regroup and reassess. And to kick her own ass for even getting all warm and fuzzy with the guy. He'd even *spooned* her the night before. And she'd liked it. She was clearly losing her edge...that, or her marbles.

No strings attached. Damn it. She dated lightly, she had fun, she did not stay the night, and she did *not* spoon. Stupid, stupid, *stupid.* Snatching her bra off the newel post, she grabbed the trailing ends of the sheet so she wouldn't trip on them and hurried down the stairs. Her clothes were right where she'd left them, piled in the living room near their discarded dinner. Except for her panties, which were still up in Price's room.

"Going somewhere?" Price's deep voice boomed like thunder above her.

Every muscle in her body locked tight, rooting her in place. *Shit. Caught.* Turning her head, she saw him leaning his forearms against the banister. The picture of casual. Except when she met his eyes. Suppressed fury simmered there. She winced and didn't bother to answer his question. They both knew where she'd been headed—out the door without a backward glance.

"You forgot something." Her lacy panties dangled from his fingertip.

"Souvenir." She smiled and tried to bravado her way out of what was turning into a sticky situation. Seriously? *Seriously?* What single man in his thirties didn't know the one-nighter protocol? If the other party wanted to bail, you weren't allowed to get upset. "Thank you for a lovely time, but I'll just be go—"

"Freeze," he barked in a voice reserved for criminals. But she froze just the same. There was no disregarding that tone.

She watched him stalk down the stairs in silence, every inch the dangerous man, the predator. It sent a thrill through her to watch him, and she stomped all over any kind of enamored feeling. That road led to ugliness and heartache. Her underwear hit the coffee table in front of her as he flung them down and crossed his arms over his chest, his muscles rippling with the movement. He wore only a pair of jeans, his damp hair sleek against his scalp.

The fact that he had any clothes on reminded her that she was still naked. She snagged her panties from where he'd dropped them and pulled them on. Then her jeans, bra, T-shirt and shoes. Okay, it was way past time to go. He watched her dress, but didn't say anything. The silence was suffocating. She sighed. "Look. I had a great time. I really did, but I can't do this."

"You *did* do this." He braced foot on the low table, and propped a forearm on his knee. The morning sun streaming through the windows played over his broad shoulders.

She dragged her gaze away from his muscles and focused on his face. "You know what I mean. I'm not interested in more that what we did last night. And this morning. I don't do serious."

"I haven't asked for anything—"

"I know. It's not your fault. It's all me." Jesus, she couldn't believe she was going to give a guy the *it's not you, it's me* speech. This was surreal. She also couldn't believe he was going to nail her for this. What guy didn't want no-strings sex? Scott sure as hell loved it with the waitresses on their restaurant staff. Her spine snapped straight at the reminder of why she didn't do complications. Her eyes narrowed. "To be blunt—"

"When aren't you?" His tone had gone *sotto voce,* and she wanted to kick him. Of course, that would put her within his arm's reach, and him getting his hands on her again was a bad idea. Very bad. A wash of heat went through her, and she studiously ignored it. She didn't want this, she didn't want him, she'd had her night of fun, he was out of her system, and it was over. Done.

It had to be. For her own good.

She crossed her arms tightly across her chest to cover the

betraying tightness of her nipples. "*To be blunt,* you're the kind of guy I could fall for. And I can't do that. I just can't. I'm sorry." That may have been an over-share, but it seemed to shut him up. Surprise flashed across his face and his mouth snapped closed so fast his teeth clacked together.

She took that as her cue to go, so she picked up her purse, walked out and didn't allow herself to look back.

Thank God she had her shop renovations to throw herself into for the rest of the day. Since she had to redo all her upholstery and repaint a wall, she'd decided to redo the earth-toned color scheme of Bean There, Done That to something more vibrant. The insurance company was paying for it, so why not do an impromptu remodel? Her new curtains and chair cushions should arrive the following week. She worked until her eyes began to cross with exhaustion. The fact that she hadn't slept the night before didn't help at all. The sun had begun to set when she finally washed out the brushes she'd used to paint. The workmen had gone home hours before.

A knock on the front door of her shop had her head popping up from where she was bent over the sink. Leaning to the side to see through the glass, she spotted Price. Her heart stuttered at the sight of him, and she groaned. Man, she had it bad. She was jonesing for him like a crack addict who'd just escaped from rehab.

Good thing she would never let it go further than one night of hot sex. She'd had to restrain herself from thinking about him today. And he had to come here and screw it up. She wondered if he'd arrest her if she ignored him. Probably. She wouldn't put it past him. He wasn't exactly a beta male. Nope, full on alpha. Too bad she liked that in her men. Someone who could match her. Not permanently, but she shouldn't have to be bored while she was dating, right?

Heat wound through her as she remembered his hands on

her skin, his body moving over hers, his lips playing against her mouth. She wanted him to go away. She wanted him to give her more. She was so fucking confused. Rubbing a tired hand down her face, she let out a shaky breath as she stepped around the counter to unlock the door.

He propped his forearm against the doorjamb and looked her over at his leisure. A shiver slid down her flesh. "Hey, sugar."

"Chief."

He straightened and walked past her into the shop. His gaze swept the interior. "You've almost got it all fixed up—it doesn't even look like there was a fire. Nice."

Her arms folded around her middle. "What are you doing here, Price? We talked this morning about how we wouldn't see each other again."

He leaned his elbows back against the countertop, crossing his legs at the ankle. "No, *you* said we wouldn't see each other again. I never agreed."

Panic skittered down her spine. "Price, please—"

"Begging is good. And I love it when you please me, Aubrey." A slow smile crossed his handsome face.

Her eyes narrowed to dangerous slits. She poked a finger towards his chest. "You know what? Just...shut up. We had a one-night stand, Chief. I'm betting it wasn't your first, and I doubt very much that it'll be your last. I told you, I don't do relationships."

He *tsked* low in his throat. "But you do more than a bunch of one-night stands. I asked around about you—"

"You *asked around?*" Her eyebrows arched and her mouth sagged open for a moment. "I live in this little hamlet, Price. People are going to talk if you start asking around about my sexual history."

He continued as though she hadn't spoken. "I asked around about you, and you've dated six men in the last few years, all for roughly two to three months. Just long enough for them to want more than sex and start making noises about wanting a real relationship. Am I getting warm?"

Her teeth ground together, but she refused to give him the satisfaction of answering. Apparently, her silence was enough for him, because a knowing smile curved his full lips. She offered him a glare in return and stomped behind the counter. Presumptuous jackass. "It doesn't matter what you think. You can't force me to date you. Or sleep with you."

"Force?" Anger sparked in his eyes as he slapped his hands on the counter and leaned toward her. "I sure as hell didn't force you to strip tease for me last night."

"And I said 'not again' this morning." Her hands planted on her hips. "No means no, Price. I'm sure you can grasp the concept."

He pushed himself upright, stalking her across the coffee shop. She backpedaled as fast as she could until she'd gone all the way into the back room and was pressed against the prep table. The heat of his big body enveloped hers, and she fought a moan. Please God, don't let him touch her again. She would *not* be able to handle it.

Bracing her hands on the prep table, she pulled herself up to sit on it. Anything to get some distance. Her body screamed for more of him. His hands, his lips, his teeth and tongue. She shuddered, heat racing through her. Her pussy clenched on nothing, and she could feel herself get slick with want. She sucked in a breath, trying to calm her pounding heart. It just drew his cologne to her. He smelled amazing, and her skin had smelled like him this morning when she woke up. His scent mixed with hers. Her nipples peaked tight, thrusting against the cotton bra she wore.

He laid his hands on the table beside her hips, his thumbs

grazing her skin through her jeans. Leaning in, his gaze met hers. "You want me."

She couldn't deny it, not when her nerves jangled with how much she needed to touch him. She folded her arms as she tried not to reach out and stroke her fingers down the hard planes of his chest. "I told you... I can't do this."

"You also said I was the kind of guy you could fall for." His lips brushed her ear, his voice taking on the low rumble that made her insides melt. "I'm the kind of guy who'd always catch you."

"Don't say things like that." Her hands fisted in his shirt, her heart stumbling. It wasn't true. It didn't matter how much she liked him or how good he was in bed, she knew how this would end if she gave too much of herself.

"I'm just telling the truth, sugar."

And then he slid one hand into her hair and kissed her. Every thought in her mind deserted her. He sucked her lower lip into his mouth, scraping her lightly with his teeth. She moaned, used her grip on his shirt to pull him closer, and wrapped her legs around his hips. Grunting, he settled against her and used his other hand to cup her ass. His hard cock rubbed her just right, grinding against her hard little clit.

Letting her head fall back, she arched into him as pleasure burned through her. He took advantage—sucking and biting a light trail of kisses down her neck. Her pussy clenched, so hot and wet she couldn't stand it. She throbbed, her nipples so hard they ached. "Price, please. I want you."

He groaned, a great shudder rippling through him. Slipping his hands to her waist, he popped the button on her pants and unfastened the zipper with a slow rasp that echoed in the wide room. "Lift your hips."

"Tell me you have a condom." She leaned back on her hands, leveraging herself up so he could pull her jeans and panties down in one swift movement.

He jerked open his slacks, magically produced a little foil package from God knew where, and had himself sheathed in record time. Which was a good thing because she didn't think she could wait. Then his mouth was on hers again, her legs were around his waist, and he was easing that long, hard cock into her slick sex. The stretch was divine, and when he began moving inside her, it was with the swift, almost punishing rhythm that she hadn't known she needed. She threw her head back, gasping.

"You're so wet, sugar. Wet and tight. I love the feel of your pussy around me." Sweat slid down his temples as his gaze caught hers. With her sitting on the table, he hit her G-spot with every single thrust. She couldn't stop a whimpering moan at his words, his movements. Everything he did made her want more.

He dipped his head and sucked her nipple into his mouth through her shirt and bra. He bit down hard enough to make her choke, to make her sex spasm. She gasped, "I love the way you touch me."

Worrying her nipple between his teeth, he chuckled when she squealed. He released her captured breast and cupped her ass in his hands, pulling her tighter to him. She had no idea how he managed it, but one fingertip teased the tight bud of her anus. She clung to his shoulders, pushing back to take him deeper into her ass. He chuckled, watching her react. "And I love touching you."

Tingles skipped down her arms and legs, waves of heat following in their wake. He barely nudged his finger in her backside as he continued to thrust his cock into her pussy and the dual sensation was enough to make her sob. The table squeaked and shuddered under their weight as they moved together, their skin slapping, their harsh breath mingling. He filled her again and again, relentless as he shoved her toward

48

the edge of orgasm. And she was right there with him, wringing him with her thighs, clenching her pussy around his cock until he groaned her name.

He ground himself against her clit, plunged his finger into her ass, and made her scream for him. Her sex convulsed, fisting on his dick as she came hard enough to make bursts of light explode behind her eyes. "Oh God, *Price.*"

"This is so fucking amazing, Aubrey," he gasped. She watched his eyes lose focus, his jaw locking as he lost himself in orgasm, pumping his long finger and cock inside her until he was spent and she was moaning helplessly with every minute movement he made within her channels.

They stayed there for a long time, their breathing gradually slowing, and their heart rates returning to normal. Only then did Price pull out of her. She shivered, sliding from the table to retrieve her jeans and redress. She could hear Price cleaning himself up and righting his clothing, but she didn't dare look at him. The man was a serious hazard to her mental health. She'd decided not to touch him again or see him again, and here she was doing him in her coffee shop not twelve hours later.

She jerked upright when his hand closed around her arm. He handed her purse to her and drew her toward the door. "W— what are you doing?"

"Taking you to dinner."

"Isn't that a little backwards?"

"So?" He moved his hand down to hers, cradling it in his big palm. It felt nice, secure. Dangerous, she warned herself. She tried to tug her hand free, but he wasn't having it. Instead, he twined his fingers with hers and squeezed hard enough to make sure she couldn't escape. Then he pulled her out the door and waited for her to use her free hand to lock up. "There's a nice diner across the square. Let's go there."

Jericho gave them a wide smile when they passed by and—

for once—had the decency not to make some crazy predictions. He kept his mouth shut and nodded to them as they passed. Price glanced at her. "Friend of yours?"

"Not exactly." Her eyebrows lifted. "Why? Are the police going to escort him out of town?"

His big shoulder rolled in a shrug. "Not unless he starts bothering people."

"He hasn't bothered me." Okay, so it wasn't true. Jericho's predictions bothered her, but before he'd started making them, they'd had no problems at all. As far as she could tell, he was just a nice old guy down on his luck.

Price nodded. "So long as he doesn't harass anyone, we're fine."

Tugging at her hand again, she frowned when his fingers tightened. His thumb stroked over her flesh and goose bumps broke over her arms. When had she ever had a reaction this strong to anyone? Never. She was in so much trouble. How could she go on a date with someone she'd just had a one-night stand and a prep table quickie with? She had no clue, but Price had her hand and he wasn't letting go, so it looked like she was about to get a crash course.

He ushered her up the steps to the little mom and pop diner next door to Celia's hair salon and snagged a booth near the back. "The town gossip says you're not from here either. Why did you come?"

"Burn out, like you. I'd had enough of the rat race after my divorce that I wanted a major change. We had all the same friends and business contacts, so I wanted out of it all." She shrugged, not bothering to look at the menu since she'd been here a million times with Celia. "I took a vacation to the coast, ended up in Mrs. Chamber's B&B...and never left."

He nodded. "I came up to visit my brother and wanted to stick around."

Mason was recruited from L.A. two years ago by some friend of a friend in the fire department. Aubrey didn't know the specifics, but she knew he was well liked by everyone. So far, everyone seemed just as impressed with Price. Interesting family. She grinned. "Your brother has a serious thing for my best friend, Celia. He goes to her salon every week to flirt with her and ask her out."

Flipping his menu closed, Price chuckled. "Mason isn't a subtle man."

"And you are?"

"We're brothers for a reason." He shrugged.

"Your dad has to be a terror."

"So was my mom. You should have met them." He chuckled softly, and they paused their conversation long enough to order when the waitress arrived.

"Should have as in past tense? What happened?"

"Car accident. They went together, which they would have wanted." Sadness darkened his gaze and it made her reach over the table and squeeze his hand. He turned his palm up and laced her fingers through his again. "It was not long after my divorce...about five years ago. When I came up to see Mason last Christmas, I realized how much I missed having family around. I talked to the former police chief about a job, found out he was retiring, and no one on the force wanted the position. So, here I am."

"Here you are." She took a sip of her water and decided to get right to the point. "Why are you pushing us dating? This isn't me playing hard to get. I don't like those kind of games."

They paused again as their order arrived. It was why she liked this place—the service was *fast* and the food was good. Price picked up his fork and his end of the conversation. "We're not going to date."

"Oh, good." Relief flooded her because at this point she

wasn't sure she had the willpower to resist if he touched her. "I'm glad we're on the same page here."

"You dump the guys you date after a few months. I'm not interested in that."

"You are so right."

He smiled. "Which is why we're just getting married."

She choked on the bite of the green beans she'd just swallowed. Her eyes watered, and she dove for her glass of water. After she'd chugged half the glass, she croaked out, "Are you out of your mind?"

"You can take as much time as you need to catch up with me on this one, but I've decided. And I'm all in. Get used to it." He leaned back in the booth and laid his arm across the back of the bench.

"We just met a week ago. This is our first real date."

His big shoulder lifted in a shrug. "When I make up my mind, I make up my mind."

"Well, you can change your mind."

"Not usually."

"*Price.*"

"You know you turn me on when you get pissed."

Her mouth gaped. "That is the most condescending, chauvinistic horseshit I have ever heard come out of a man's mouth. And it's fucking trite on top of that."

"I still have a serious hard-on right now. It's not something I can control."

She sputtered for a second before she offered him a nasty glare. "You did that on purpose to try and get me to stop talking about how you're *insane* to want to *marry* me on the second date. The first real out-of-the-house date."

"Well, I might have mentioned this yesterday but you saw fit to strip naked. There was no way in hell I was letting you get sidetracked by anything. And I'd have told you this morning, but you ran out." He took a swig of his coffee. "I might have to spank you for that later."

Fire exploded in her veins at the thought of his hand on her upturned ass. *Holy shit.* She just stared at him, heat flooding her cheeks. Her breathing hitched, and her hands clenched on the tabletop.

He met her gaze, his golden skin stretching taut over his sharp cheekbones. "Stop looking at me like that, sugar. I'm not fucking you again until you see things my way."

"Then you're not fucking me again."

He just grinned. "We'll see about that."

"This is insane." She tapped her fork against her plate agitatedly. "Do you really think it's that simple to make a relationship out of thin air?"

"I knew you the moment I met you. End of story. I know it sounds crazy, but that's how it is." His heavy brows snapped together. "You think that's easy for me to admit?"

"You make it sound easy." She shifted uncomfortably. Hadn't she thought that the first day they'd met? That she *knew* him...that she *liked* him?

"I'm divorced too, sugar. Don't forget that. I've got a couple of scars of my own in the relationship department. I just haven't written all women off."

"I haven't written men off." But her protest sounded weak even to her own ears.

He arched an eyebrow. "You don't think so?"

"I date."

A derisive snort was his answer.

Uncertainty crawled through her. She was honest enough to admit she *had* written men off, but it sounded so much more cowardly when he said it that way, like she didn't have a good reason to be leery of relationships...of men. "I don't have to want to get married again. There's nothing wrong with me if I want to be single."

"Yeah, if you wanted to be single. You're just scared."

Anger simmered deep inside her, a knee-jerk reaction after being dicked around so badly in her last relationship. "Drop. Dead."

"It's not going to make it untrue if you get mad." He offered up a smirk. "But go ahead, sugar. You know how much I like it."

The shriek that escaped her sounded like a whistling teakettle. Her hands fisted tightly and she had to think really hard about how stupid it would be to assault a police officer. Especially the Chief of Police. She tried to remind herself about how she was too pretty for jail, and about how much he would enjoy it and smirk some more if he got to lock her in a cell. That mellowed her right out. No way in hell would she give him the satisfaction. She bared her teeth in a smile. "Well, since we're playing by your rules now, you can get as turned on as you want, *sugar*, but you're still not getting laid because I'm not *seeing things your way* any time soon."

His mouth opened and closed. He narrowed his eyes at her, and now it was her turn to smirk. He deserved it for making her wait. He wanted strings attached to his sex? Fine. He got to dance around like Pinocchio then.

Of course, she was dancing alongside his stubborn ass. *Damn it.*

"Well, this is going to be interesting." He grinned, challenge sparking in his gaze. "Finish your dinner."

Because she didn't have a clue what else to say to him, she did as he said. They finished their meal in silence, her insides churning so much that she just picked at her food. The waitress dropped off the check, he plopped down a few bills to cover the tab and stood. It left her eye-level with his groin, and she got a good enough look to tell her he hadn't been lying about the erection. Her mouth watered needing a taste. She hadn't sucked him last night, and she wanted to. He folded her hand in his and tugged her to her feet and out the door. "Come on. I'll walk you home."

Chapter Four

Three weeks later, she still hadn't convinced him that more sex was a good idea. No, a *great* idea. The man drove her up the wall, and she loved every minute of it. Damn him. She liked him more every moment she spent with him. He was everything she'd thought he was that first day—strong, steady, dependable—and a hell of a lot more. He made her laugh, he made her want, he made her crazy. That didn't mean she was going to roll over and marry him because he said so. She still didn't believe she was cut out for marriage, but she'd certainly like to roll over and do a lot of other things with him.

He'd dragged her out on a lot of non-dates—because he insisted they weren't dating—and, on the fifth one, she'd talked him inside her apartment. In under thirty seconds, he'd had her pressed up against her living room wall, his tongue in her mouth and his hand up her skirt, stroking her through her soaking panties.

"I want you."

"I want you too, sugar."

And he still wouldn't give in. The man had a will of absolute steel. It was unfair. She growled low in her throat. "Fine," she spat. "I guess you're right that we're...in a *relationship*."

"Not good enough, sugar." A smile kicked up one side of his mouth, and he shook his head down at her. "You know what it'll take to—"

Her jaw clenched, and she tried to jerk away from him. "Since we're not doing anything else tonight, you can see your way out."

He chuckled. "Oh, but that was very good, Aubrey. Definite progress. I think you deserve a reward."

"Wh—what do you mean by *reward*?" Wariness and hope twisted inside her. God, she was so hard up she couldn't take much more. And neither could her vibrator. If she spent another night working herself over with it, it was going to give up the ghost.

His big hands cupped her hips as he sank to his knees. He slipped his fingers under her skirt and hooked into the top of her panties. His green gaze, hard with lust, never left hers as he slid the silk down to her ankles. "Step out of them."

She lifted her feet one at a time to let him pull them all the way off. He grinned and tucked them in his pocket. "I never did get my souvenir."

"You can have my whole underwear drawer if you fuck—" Her mind shut down when his fingers thrust deep into her pussy. *Oh. Holy. God.*

His free hand slid up her thigh. She loved his touch on her skin, the slight calluses on his finger rasped over her sensitive flesh. It was amazing. Her skirt bunched around her thighs when he pulled her leg up and over his broad shoulder, opening her wide. His lips brushed the inside of her knee. She whimpered, heat whipping through her body. Her pussy was so slick, she could feel the excess moisture slip down her legs.

He licked a path up the inside of her thigh, catching the beads of wetness with his hot tongue. She moaned, clenching her fingers in his hair. Anticipation made her muscles shake, and her heartbeat thundered in her ears until she couldn't hear anything else.

God, she'd waited so long for this, wanted it so badly.

His tongue dipped into her pussy, flicking over the wet labia. She choked when he closed his mouth over her clit and sucked hard. His fingers moved inside her, stroking fast and deep. Heat roared through her, tingles racing over her flesh in waves. Her pussy clenched around his thrusting digits, and she closed her eyes to feel her body tighten. She was close.

Hooking his fingers in her sex, he hit her in just the right spot to make her scream his name. He bit at her pulsing clit, and it was enough, more than enough, to shove her over into orgasm. Her pussy flexed, and her hips slapped against the wall as she arched toward the wicked talent of his mouth and fingers. She threw her head back and choked on a harsh sob. Oh, *God.* The muscles of her thighs jerked, and her breath bellowed out in rough pants. She shuddered over and over as the orgasm kept going.

When it finally ended, she collapsed in his arms, and he hugged her close to his broad chest. She straddled his lap, and she could feel the hot press of his cock between her legs. He was hard for her, and she wanted him so much. His tongue hadn't been enough. She wanted *more.* She shivered as she remembered what it felt like to have his dick push into her sex. Yes. She needed that.

She planted a hand on his chest, pushing him flat. Moving her hand down his torso, she cupped his cock through his jeans. His hands locked around her wrists, stilling her movements. "Aubrey."

Licking her lips, she gave him a grin she hoped would make him think of nothing but sex. Just the way she was. "It's not sex. It's a *reward.*"

"Shit." He threw his arm over his eyes.

Flicking the tab on his jeans, she jerked the zipper open. No underwear, as usual. His heavy cock slipped free into her hand. He groaned when she touched him, stroked him. She wriggled down his hard body until she could lick the underside of his dick from base to tip. "Look at me. I want you to watch me."

His arm dropped away until he could meet her gaze. The emerald fire that burned in his eyes made her nipples harden, made her pussy flash hot and wet again. She had to squeeze her thighs together for a moment to contain a harsh throb of want. "Aubrey, I—"

She grinned and sucked the length of him into her mouth. His fingers fisted in her hair, tugging on the long strands. The slight pain made her scalp throb, but it shot sensations straight to her pussy. She loved sucking cock, it was the headiest power trip she'd ever experienced. But with Price, it was something more. It wasn't just the power of having him at her mercy, she was so turned on her pussy contracted with every thrust of his cock into her mouth. Her cheeks hollowed with every hard pull on his dick. Her own wetness increased when she tasted the pre-cum that beaded from the plum-shaped head. She moaned on his cock, fire building higher and higher in her pussy until she couldn't bear it. His fingers clenched tighter in her hair, using his grip for leverage as his hips arched. She worked her hands and mouth up and down his hard cock, sucking him deep until he touched the back of her throat. He groaned, his hips lifted and he froze. His come jetted into her throat, and her pussy flexed on nothing as she came with him. She whimpered as they shuddered together, fire and ice streaking over her skin. Her eyes closed tight and tears leaked down her cheeks. Jesus, it had never been that intense for her before. She swallowed and pulled back to curl on to her side away from him. What the hell had just happened?

She clamped a hand over her mouth to hold back a sob. Emotion she couldn't even begin to handle rolled through her. Price's hand closed over her shoulder, but she resisted. "Please go away."

"Aubrey—sugar—did I hurt you? What's wrong?" An edge of panic rasped in his voice.

Curling deeper into herself, she tried to shut him out. "No,

I'm fine."

"Like hell." He pushed his arm under her and rolled her to face him. She buried her face in his shoulder and cried in earnest, sobs shaking her whole body. He didn't demand to know what was wrong, didn't get pissed when she kept crying. No, he cradled her to his chest like she was the most precious thing in his life. It made her sob harder, and she wrapped her arms around his neck and held him tight.

She didn't even know why she was crying. If he'd asked, she couldn't have told him. It was everything, and nothing, and...she couldn't even begin to describe this huge ball of emotion that ballooned in her chest when he was near. Taking it all in was more than she could deal with. Her sobs slowed, but tears still leaked from the corners of her eyes. Her chest hitched with every breath, and she pulled out of it enough to notice he'd settled her on his lap and was crooning to her the way he would a terrified child. It wasn't even words, but it comforted her and she relaxed by degrees until she curled limply against him. She swiped the back of her hand over her cheeks. "I, um, I'm sorry. I don't norm—"

"Shh." He rested his chin on the top of her head, his hand stroking up and down her back. It made her eyes well with tears again, and she blinked fast to hold them back. What was wrong with her? This wasn't normal. Nothing like this had ever happened to her, not even with Scott. And she'd been head over heels for him. But look how well that ended. God, she was so confused. Price brushed her hair back and kissed her forehead. A shiver ran down her spine. She thought she'd react to the man if she was on death's doorstep. It was madness.

His hand continued rubbing her back in soothing circles. "Are you all right, sugar?"

She swallowed and nodded, too hollowed out by the firestorm of emotion she'd just spent to care that he'd seen her sob like a baby. She moved to rise, but he held her to him, shifting her in his arms so he could stand. He walked down the hall until he found her bedroom and laid her on the soft sheets. With quick efficiency, he stripped her and then stepped back. She closed her eyes so she didn't have to watch him walk away like she had almost every night for the last three weeks. She couldn't do it, not tonight.

The mattress dipped as he settled beside her. Her eyes flew open, and she found that he'd shed his own clothes too. He pulled her to him so that they were plastered together from knee to chest. Her breasts crushed to his pecs and her nipples went so hard it was painful. She swallowed a moan when she felt his cock curve against her belly.

Angling a glance up at him, she shivered at the lust that always shone in his eyes. For her. "But you have a no-sex rule."

"You're worth breaking every damn rule, sugar."

Burying her fingers in his hair, she pulled him down until she could kiss him. His lips brushed over hers with a reverence she'd never experienced before. He lifted her leg so that it hooked over his hip. Tingles slipped over her skin, and she pressed closer. The head of his cock nudged at the swollen lips of her sex. She wanted him, her body molding itself to him. But this time, it wasn't a wild race to the finish, it was a slow burn that simmered from inside out.

His cock sank deep inside her with one hot, unhurried push. She sighed, enjoying the clasp of her flesh around him, the pull of desire that tugged at her very soul. It was perfect. Just the thought should panic her, but she was beyond caring about anything except savoring this moment with him. Price. His name rolled through her mind with the drugging sweetness of aged whiskey. She hummed in the back of her throat as their tongues danced.

Their hips rocked together and time became fluid, the slow throb of desire clenched her muscles. She pulled back to gasp out a breath, her muscles shook with suppressed longing. He cupped her ass, sliding his fingers forward to tease the lips of her pussy from behind. She moaned when he circled her anus. His gaze locked with hers and she felt orgasm build within her, but she held it off and held it off, wanting to stay in this place with him. His smile told her he knew what she was doing, the way his gaze sharpened told her he fought coming as well. A laugh caught her by surprise, and he smiled at her. "Price, I—"

She cried out when his thick finger penetrated her ass, stretching her anus in time with his thrusting cock. She tumbled hard and fast over the edge of orgasm, the walls of her sex closing on his dick in rhythmic contractions. Her nails dug into his shoulders as she rode out the hot waves of pleasure that threatened to drag her under. She wanted to see his face when he came.

He groaned, rolling his pelvis against hers. Aftershocks of orgasm rippled through her and her pussy tightened around him. His beautiful eyes lost focus, and his fingers worked inside her ass while he slammed his cock into her one more time. His breath hissed out, his come filling her. He shuddered against her, pulling her closer until his arms wrapped around her. A few moments passed while they both tried to catch their breath. He leaned back to look at her, a smile that was sinfully wicked curving his lips. He pushed his fingers deeper into her backside. "It occurs to me that I owe you a spanking."

The sound that emerged from her throat was half moan and half laugh. Just like that, she was hot and eager for him. Needy. This man got to her like nothing else ever had. "You did promise me. Time to pay up."

"I am a man of my word." He slid his cock and fingers out of her, wrapped his arm around her waist, and had her facedown on his lap before she could blink.

She tossed a sassy grin over her shoulder at him. Her heart pounded, and her hands shook so hard she had to bunch them in the sheets. The mere thought of his hand on her ass was enough to make her wet. She couldn't wait. "Give me your best shot, Chief."

"You're in for it now, sugar." He laughed and the sound wrapped around her heart, making her smile widen. Cupping his hand over her buttocks, he rubbed slow circles on her flesh that built her anticipation to a boiling point.

She lifted her backside into his stroking palm and waited for the first strike to land. He didn't disappoint her. The blow cracked loudly in the quiet room, the echo a shock that made her gasp. Heat and ecstatic pain flowed in the wake of the startling sound. He smacked her other cheek, and she moaned, rocking into his hand. Raining slaps that varied between punishing spanks and playful pats, he kept her off-guard. Dark pleasure wound tight within her, centering in her sex until her pussy clenched with every swat. She undulated on his lap, letting go of every ounce of control as she let him take her to a sweet, hot place that was pure sensation.

Moaning, she buried her face in the mattress, not sure how much more she could take before she begged him to fuck her. "P—Price, I need more."

"God, sugar. You get me hard more often than a horny teenager." He pulled her upright on his lap until she straddled his thighs, but faced away from him. The blunt tip of his cock probed her anus, and she threw her head back, bowing her neck over his shoulder as she arched in utter abandon. His arm circled her hips and pressed her down to take his painful penetration. But she was already beyond pleasure and pain, the two had become one, twisting together until all she wanted was *more*.

"*Oooh*." She rocked herself against him, working herself slowly on his cock. Closing her eyes, she bit her lip and focused on the rising tide of sensation. He fitted his hands to her waist, lifting and lowering her, stretching her with each thrust. It was so good, so hot. His rougher flesh stimulated her swollen

63

backside, his hard belly spanking against her ass as their movements picked up speed and force. The muscles in her thighs screamed with strain, sweat sliding down their bodies to seal their skin together where it touched.

She wrapped her fingers around his wrists, digging her nails in as she used her grip for leverage to quicken the pace. Each time he entered her ass, her sex throbbed. She could feel her orgasm building, coalescing into something sharp and shattering.

"Please," she begged. She didn't know what she pleaded for. For it to end. For it to never end.

"Aubrey." His voice was ragged, his chest heaving, but his tone still managed to be reverent. He kissed the side of her neck. "Aubrey."

Slipping one hand down, he flicked his fingertip over her clit. She sobbed, so close to orgasm she could taste its sweetness, but unable to move fast enough to push herself over the edge. He pulled her down tightly to him, grinding his pelvis against her punished ass. The penetration was deeper than any that had come before, widening her anus past bearing. God, it was so fucking good. Then he pinched her clit and bit the side of her neck. Hard.

She flipped over into orgasm so fast it left her gasping. Her ass closed around his cock, her pussy clenching on nothingness as he worked her clit and dragged her release out for as long as possible. He pumped into her ass over and over again, coming hard inside her, filling her with hot fluids that made her shudder.

Catching her as she collapsed against him, he rolled them until he lay on his back and she sprawled on his chest. She yawned, exhaustion sweeping through her, the emotional and sexual rollercoaster she'd been on taking its toll. Her heart tripped when he cuddled her close and brushed his lips across her forehead.

Her eyes closed, and she kissed his collarbone before sleep took her. Nothing had ever felt as good as this, been as achingly intense as this. Nothing. She never wanted this *feeling* to end. She just wanted to stay right here forever.

Split shifts sucked. She'd finally gotten permission from the building inspector to reopen Bean There, Done That, and business was booming since every cop and fireman in town now insisted on stopping by at least once a day. Price and Mason were a force to be reckoned with in Cedarville. She'd opened the shop that morning and now she had to close it down for the night. Owner or not, if a split shift had to be worked, it was usually her who did it. Her staff was trying to juggle hours until Susan got back on her feet. She was supposed to come in tomorrow. Thank God.

But finally six o'clock rolled around, and it was quitting time. Aubrey cleaned all the equipment, wiped down the counters and headed out the side door. Price had called to tell her something was up at work, and he'd be late. She frowned. While she was okay with work being important, a nagging worry went through her. Cedarville wasn't L.A., so the dangers of his job would be much less than if he still lived there, but bad things happened even in small towns. He'd promised her he'd be careful, and she had to trust that he would. Which was tough for her, but she did trust that he knew how to do his job. And that wasn't the only thing he knew how to do.

Post-coital bliss was the understatement of the century. Jesus, Price was great in bed. She didn't know if he was more skilled than any of her other lovers, or just the chemistry between them was better that she'd ever experienced before. Or both. Or...hell, she didn't really care so long as he kept her coming like clockwork. All. Night. Long.

A delicious shiver went down her spine. She could get used to this. She'd never clicked with anyone this deeply, this fast. It was terrifying and exhilarating and she knew she had the stupidest grin on her face and didn't even care, but it faded as quickly as it had formed.

The other worry she'd been suppressing all day came back to her in a rush now that she didn't have her own work to distract her. Price and she had had sex last night without a condom. And she hadn't dated anyone in almost a year, so she wasn't on the pill. Terror and panic should be careening through her...but they weren't. *That* was what freaked her out a little. It wasn't that she didn't want kids. She'd always wanted a couple of them before she'd gotten married, but the idea of breeding with Scott had always made her a little wary. He was a selfish man, she'd just never realized how selfish. Until it was over.

But...would having *Price's* child be that terrible? Well, she wasn't having a heart attack at the thought, and that said something right there. She was so wrapped up in her own thoughts, she didn't even notice Jericho until he grabbed her.

His fingers wrapped around her arms in a tight grip, desperation in his silver gaze. She'd never noticed before how brilliant the color of his eyes were. "You must save your soul mate. Now. You don't have a moment to lose, Aubrey."

She stared at him. Creepy nutso boy was back.

"You have to believe, Aubrey. You have to believe in something."

Her heart gave a hard thump, and her worry for Price over his job came roaring back. Her stomach gave a vicious twist. So far Jericho hadn't been wrong. Not once. Did she really believe in what he said enough to go tearing across town in search of Price? And what if she didn't and something bad happened to him? Her chest squeezed tight, and for a moment she couldn't breathe. Something bad could happen to Price. Oh, God.

The truth slammed into her in one unholy wave of terror.

She was in love with Price, and there was no way in hell she was taking any chances with his safety. She'd rather look insane running around town after him than let anything happen to him.

Jericho shook her hard. "14 Plumleigh Avenue, on the corner of Larkspur. Believe me, Aubrey. *Go!*"

She went, her legs and arms pumping as she raced across the square and over the five blocks to get to the address Jericho had given her. Her breath rasped out in painful pants. If this had to do with Price's job, he would kill her for interfering. Did she care? Not really. He could kick her ass if it meant he was alive, breathing and healthy enough to get it done.

She skidded to a stop outside of 14 Plumleigh. The front window was broken out, the roof sagged on the porch, and the house looked as if it should be condemned. Her breath whooshed out in relief when she saw Price, alive and well, through the broken window. He wore a black bulletproof vest as he walked down a dark hallway toward the back of the house. She swallowed, blinking back tears.

Thank God, Jericho was wrong.

Through her tears she saw a slim man step into the hall behind Price. He wasn't wearing a uniform and he carried a silver pistol. Her breath seized when he lifted the weapon to point it at Price's unprotected head.

"Price, *behind you!*"

Both men spun toward her at the same time, guns raised. She dropped to the pavement and covered her head with her arms. The cement scraped the skin off her elbows and knees. Two deafening booms echoed over the quiet street, and she flinched, curling tighter into herself. Please, God, don't let Price be hurt. Please, God, let her have warned him in time. Please, God. Please, God. *Please, God.*

Her ears buzzed, and her whole body shook as shock

rocketed through her system. She needed to get up and check if Price was okay, but the message her brain was sending to her quivering muscles didn't seem to be getting through. She panted against the cement, small rocks and dirt rubbing against her cheek.

"*Aubrey.*"

Relief flooded her system as she heard Price's voice shout from a distance. A very far off distance. It sounded like he was yelling from the end of a long tunnel. Tingles broke down her arms as someone grabbed her and flipped her over.

Price's face hung over her, abject terror drawing the skin tight over his cheekbones. His big hands slid over her body in efficient movements. "Aubrey, are you hurt?"

"No, I'm fine." Though her tone sounded vague and soft to her ears. She shook her head to try to clear it. Swallowing, she laid a hand along his jaw. "Are *you* all right?"

"Hell, no. I'm not all right." Molten rage flashed in his gaze and the muscles in his jaw clenched beneath her fingers. His hands shook as they brushed the dirt off her cheek. "What were you thinking yelling like that? It was crazy amounts of stupid."

Matching anger whipped through her, stripping away the strange lethargy that weighed down her limbs. She pulled away from him and sat up, poking a finger into his chest. "I was thinking that I was saving you from getting shot. Excuse the hell out of me if that was *stupid*. My mistake."

"That wasn't what I—"

Pushing to her feet, she swayed a bit and he caught her against his chest. She wanted to stay there in his arms forever. Where they were both safe and okay. Her heart turned over, and she had to close her eyes. The anger drained away as quickly as it had come.

"Chief, I—" Another man spoke from behind her, but he cut himself off. "Never mind, I'll ask Sergeant Barkum."

She blew out a breath and forced herself to step away from Price. "So, I'll...um...see you tonight. If you have time, of course."

He sighed, reluctantly letting her go. "One of my men is going to have to ask you about what you saw and did."

"Oh, fun." She rolled her eyes to hide the tears of relief. "I just love doing police reports."

Sergeant Barkum ended up taking her statement, and for once in her life, she lied to an officer of the law. What was she going to do? Tell them she had her own personal homeless oracle? She played the shocked, confused, didn't-remember-a-thing card for all it was worth. She consoled her guilty conscience by reminding herself she'd done nothing illegal to find out Price was here and in danger.

When the sergeant finally finished with her, she turned to leave only to be drawn up short when Price called her name. He gave her an odd look. "Mrs. Chambers says she saw you running like a crazy woman through town. How were you going for a run down this street and just happened to see me?"

"I told the officer, I honestly don't remember. I was at my shop and then I was here and then there were bullets."

"You're in sandals—not the best jogging shoes."

"Look, I know it's weird. But just trust me...it's what I remember. I don't know why I went running." She laid a hand on his chest. "I don't know why I came here, but I'm glad I did if you're okay."

"Aubrey..." Suspicion faded from his eyes, replaced by warmth. He tugged her into his arms, and she went. She didn't even mind the bulletproof vest. This was exactly where she wanted to be.

"I'm sorry I don't remember more." *I'm sorry I have to lie so you don't think I'm insane.* But would they believe that a vagabond prophet sent her to save the day? She wouldn't in

69

their place. Price was fine and that was all that mattered. She'd play the amnesiac if she had to. Maybe on their fiftieth wedding anniversary, she'd tell him the truth about what happened today. Fifty sounded like a nice round number to her.

"I love you, Aubrey."

"I love you too." Taking a breath, she pulled back to look him in the eyes. She loved the way they crinkled at the corners when he smiled at her. "Price—"

"Yeah, sugar?"

"Will you marry me?"

He blinked. "Yes."

"That's it?"

"What's it?"

"Just yes? No questions or doubts or...anything?" He'd been saying he wanted to marry her since their first date—or was it technically their second date? She had no idea—but after more time around her, she'd figured he'd need some serious convincing. Scott had—she shut down that line of thinking. If there was one thing she knew, it was that Scott would never be a fraction of the man Price was. No more comparing them.

"Not one." He slid his fingers into the pocket of his slacks and pulled out a ring with a sapphire surrounded by diamonds. "I've been carrying this thing around for weeks." He grinned, and it was the most beautiful thing she'd ever seen. "We should get married in the park, what do you think?"

Tears welled up in her eyes, and all she could do was nod. He slid the ring on her finger and then lifted her hand to his lips, turned it over, and kissed her palm. "I love you."

"I know it." He smiled. "I love you too, sugar."

And she believed him.

She had to thank Jericho.

Price wanted her to go back to his place and wait for him there. She would, but not until she tracked down Jericho and thanked him up one side and down the other. Cold sweat broke out on her forehead when she thought about what might have happened to Price if Jericho hadn't sent her to save him. Where was he? Jericho was always sitting on the park bench across from her coffee shop. Always. His butt had been glued there for months now.

She jogged up to the bench to find his sign leaning up against it. But no Jericho. Shading her eyes, she looked up and down the block. Maybe he needed to use the john, and he'd be right back. Fifteen minutes later, she was sitting in his usual spot. Nothing. He was never away from the bench this long, and a twist of worry cramped her belly. Where was he? Glancing down at the sign, she saw a hand-written note scrawled in the corner. *What the hell?*

Picking up the sign, she brought it up to her nose so she could read it. Underneath the huge words "The End is Near" was *Gone to save another lost soul, Your Guardian Angel.*

She choked on a laugh, but for the third time in one day, she believed.

Believe in Me

Dedication

This one is for my editor, Bethany Morgan, who read the prequel and said, "Jericho must have his own story. No, really. I'm not kidding. Write Jericho's story." And so it was and so it is.

Chapter One

Cedarville, Oregon

Not all people need a guardian angel to find their soul mate. Then again, not all people *have* a soul mate. Guardians are only assigned to the ones who needed a little extra guidance, a push, some encouragement.

In other words, Tori Chambers worked with the lost causes. The stubborn, bitter, damaged, scarred, wary pains in the backside who needed to have a cattle-prod taken to them in order to get them into a headspace where they might actually fall for their soul mate. In ideal circumstances, only one of the two soul mates needed the help of a Guardian.

She was not currently operating under ideal circumstances. No, this assignment was a total bitch.

Hitching herself into a chair at the one and only beauty salon Cedarville had to offer, Tori dug a magazine out of her enormous handbag and began flipping through pages while she ran the details of this hellish job through her mind. She had a never-married-but-three-times-engaged and thrice-burned firefighter whom she'd been doing her level best to prod, cajole, kick and encourage to hook up with a twice-divorced hairstylist.

Mason Delacroix and Celia Occam.

Tori was holding up her end of the bargain, and for the first time she was damn thankful for having a stubborn client, because once Mason had decided he was interested, he'd latched on like a terrier and refused to let go. The problem was he was just determined to get in his soul mate's pants. He had no desire for a relationship, and there wasn't going to *be* a relationship if Celia's Guardian didn't get off her ass and do her job. It had been a *year* and Celia hadn't budged in her refusal to even consider a date with Mason.

Desperation twisted deep inside Tori. How much longer would she get before this assignment was considered a failure by the Powers That Be? Her belly looped into an even tighter knot. She couldn't fail. She just couldn't. With what happened to Guardians after they'd failed...

Fuck. Tori bit back the urge to spew the curse aloud, along with a few other creative, spleen-venting invectives. People would be horrified if old Mrs. Chambers ripped loose with the kind of swear words that Tori wanted to use. If she had known she'd be stuck in this little 'burb so long, she wouldn't have played a gossipy old biddy. At the time, she'd needed to be someone Mason wouldn't be interested in, so the role fit. Now, she just wanted to look like herself again for five whole minutes. She also wanted to get laid again, but a harmless old lady wouldn't have the kind of all night long stamina Tori did, which was at least what it would take to burn off the frustration of months and months of no sex.

She crossed her legs to squelch the need she couldn't do a damn thing about and flipped another page in the magazine while she waited for the new stylist at Occam's Razor to come fix her hair. Not that she cared about the white bun that coiled around her head. She was here to witness round one million in the battles of the sexes, when Mason had his weekly appointment with Celia to get his head shaved. He had a face and body that would put Vin Diesel to shame, and Tori had no idea how the woman had managed to hold out this long. She was ready to jump him herself. A sigh eased past her lips. As if she would. Guardians were strictly forbidden from fraternizing with their clients, and that went double for Guardians like Tori who influenced matters of the heart. However, other humans and other angels were fair game.

Unfortunately, the humans who would be interested in old Mrs. Chambers weren't exactly lighting Tori's fire. She wrinkled her nose.

A sharply drawn breath dragged her gaze up to the mirror, and she saw the reflection of a man frozen just behind and to the side of her. A man so flamingly gay, she had to bite her lip to hold back a grin. He was really working the stereotype in an over-the-top kind of way. Knee-high boots, tight silver pants and a black button-up shirt that hugged his painfully skinny body. He even wore eyeliner to make his silver eyes stand out.

Those eyes. God, she knew those eyes.

The hairs rose on the back of her neck, and she slowly turned her head to stare at a man who looked nothing like his reflection. Looking directly at him, she could see through the glamour that Guardians showed the world. She could see the man, the Guardian, as he truly was. Tall, broad, muscular, with dark hair that was just a little too long, and a face that was just a little too craggy to be handsome. But those eyes. Deep unfathomable silver pools. They were powerful, compelling, magnetic. They dragged at something deep inside her, wrenching at her very bones.

"Vitoria," he rasped. He rolled the "r" in the traditional Spanish pronunciation of her name, just the way he had the first day she'd met him over a century and a half ago. He'd even managed to keep the soft twang of his Texas accent.

God help her. Not him. *Anyone* but him.

"Jericho."

Chapter Two

"Jerry, you know Mrs. Chambers?" Celia's head cocked to the side as she studied them.

The world snapped back into focus, and Jericho shook himself. He glanced in the mirror, taking in Tori's altered appearance. Looking directly at her, he would have been able to see through her glamour as easily as she'd seen through his. For him, there would be wide amber eyes, long ebony hair, and golden skin rather than the pale features of Mrs. Chambers.

He flapped a dismissive hand at the other stylist, working the gay angle like nobody's business. "Oh, the two of us go way back, don't we, sweetness?"

"Yeah. Jerry." Tori almost grinned at his performance before his long, calloused fingers lifted to slide her hair out of its knot. The smile died before it fully formed, and she tensed to still the automatic shiver of pleasure that wanted to ripple through her.

No. A thousand times no. She was not going down that road again. It was because of *him* that she'd been stuck a Guardian for more decades than she cared to count. Hell, it was because of him that she'd died in the first place. Because she'd loved him and he'd just used her for sex, for revenge against her brother, for any number of reasons he'd never bothered to share with her, but none of them were the love she'd craved.

"Go out with me this weekend." Mason's deep voice yanked Tori out of her unpleasant trip along memory lane. He flashed his most charming smile at Celia, who didn't so much as pause before she shot him down. The woman was on autopilot.

Shaking her out of that would be tough, but from the look of things, that was Jericho's problem now. Tori sighed.

Celia kept her gaze glued to the razor she was using to scrape away the stubble on Mason's head. "No can do, champ. I'm leaving tomorrow for a hair show and won't be back for a week. Jerry can give you your regularly scheduled scalping while I'm gone."

Mason cast Jericho a disgruntled look, and the other man just shrugged, swirled a silver cape around Tori's shoulders, and then continued to fuss with her hair.

"She's leaving?" Tori hissed, frustrated at yet another delay in a long line of them. At least this time she could take it out on someone. If anyone deserved her ire, it was Jericho. "How is this you doing your job?"

"Absence makes the heart grow fonder," he murmured. "And you could try believing in me, for once. I know what I'm doing."

Any response she might have made died on her lips when his rough fingertips slid against her skull, and her involuntary shiver couldn't be quelled this time. Her heart slammed against her ribcage, her lungs seizing as her long-denied hormones rioted. Heat and lust spun through her so fast it left her reeling, and all he was doing was gliding his fingers through her hair.

She cursed herself for a fool as she silently struggled against the pull he had on her. The struggle was a dismal failure. Her nipples hardened to thrust against her bra, and she crossed her legs tighter, but it did nothing to stop the empty ache that throbbed between her thighs. She could feel herself growing wet, the folds of her sex swelling. Sucking in a deep breath to try to calm her racing heart and slow her erratic breathing, she only managed to draw in his scent over the fumes of salon chemicals. The hot, masculine smell of him was so familiar, even after all this time, and the realization sent a harsh pang through her.

His fingertips moved down to work the tension out of her neck, and she swallowed a moan. Her body softened for him, some muscles loosening while others tightened to ready her for sex. Helpless anger roared within her, and she pinched her eyes closed in denial of one simple truth. If he ever *tried* to seduce her, she was fucked. In every possible way.

Just like she had been so long ago.

He leaned forward to grab a pair of scissors off of the counter in front of the chair and his lips brushed her ear. "Think of it this way, Celia being gone gives us a week to formulate a game plan."

The last thing she wanted was to spend time with him, but the faster they got Mason and Celia together, the faster she could escape from Cedarville. And him. "Fine."

"Dinner tonight? To discuss plans?" His scent filled her lungs, and the need within her twisted tighter. Damn fate for doing this to her, for shoving her back into contact with the last man in the world she wanted to see. Ever.

"I'll meet you next door." A little diner occupied the space next to the hair salon. It had good food and, more importantly, booths that offered enough privacy for them to talk without being overheard. Anyone who listened in would think they were batshit nutty anyway, but it was best not to draw attention to themselves. Humans just wouldn't understand. Back when she'd *been* a human, she wouldn't have understood either, so she couldn't blame them.

His hands began expertly snipping away at her hair, trimming the ends and letting them flutter in tufts to the floor. She'd bet her afterlife he'd never cut hair before. That was how things worked as a Guardian. If you needed a skill for an assignment, it just came to you. If you wanted to look a certain way, you just did. There were no wings, no halo, no white light, no awe-inspiring powers. Maybe because the human-born angels were the lowest rung on the celestial corporate ladder, but maybe not. They didn't even have a superior they answered to—they were merely *compelled* to do the jobs they did. They woke up one day, their heads filled with the assignment at hand. And then they went to work. There was no fighting it, no trying to get out, no rebellion. This was what they'd been called upon to do, and they'd do it until they failed to get it right. End of story.

"All right, that should do it." He brushed a few stray strands off the cape. His silver eyes met hers briefly in the mirror, and awareness she didn't want to feel tingled down her spine. "I get off at seven."

The words *get off* falling from his lips did nothing to calm her rabbiting heartbeat. "Until seven, then."

Jericho was waiting for her when she arrived at the restaurant, his big body dominating one of the tall wooden booths in the back. His long fingers toyed idly with the silverware in front of him.

"Mrs. Chambers, it's good to see you!" One of the waitresses offered a big smile as Tori stepped in from the door.

"Thanks, Lindsay. How's your mom doing?" The girl's mother had recently broken up with her boyfriend, and as the resident town gossip, it was Tori's job to make sure everyone knew she knew their business. This definitely wasn't a position she'd have wanted for a whole year. She felt twinges of guilt whenever she spread people's news around, but she had to keep up her cover.

"Mom's doing okay. I guess."

Lindsay's smile wobbled a bit and Tori gave her arm a comforting pat. "It'll all turn out all right. You mark my words, young lady."

"Thanks, Mrs. Chambers." The girl pulled in a big breath and her grin became more genuine. "Where would you like to sit?"

"Oh, I'm meeting a friend for dinner." Tori glanced up and found Jericho's sharp gaze pinned to her, taking in the exchange between the two women. She cleared her throat and tilted her head towards his booth. "Bring us both the special and some coffee, would you?"

"Sure thing, Mrs. Chambers." Lindsay moved to obey while Tori approached the booth, sliding onto the bench opposite her worst mistake.

"Vitoria," he said in greeting.

"It's just Tori now." Unlike him, she'd done everything in her power to ditch her accent, her old identity. The rolling Spanish inflection had made her stand out in the United States when she'd needed to blend in. She rarely spoke her native tongue anymore—not unless an assignment called for it. Her job was her life now. She didn't need to be a beautiful, accomplished young lady any longer. There was no rich, doting husband to attract, no parties to host at her older brother's *hacienda*. A pang of longing went through her. She missed Enrique so much—her only family after their parents had passed away. They'd been devoted to each other, so much so that she'd insisted on accompanying him in 1836 when he rode with Santa Anna from Mexico to fight against the rebellious American settlers in Texas.

Rebellious settlers like Jericho.

So long ago, and yet she recalled every detail of that time as if it had been branded into her mind.

Lindsay glided up carrying a big tray, lowering it to the tabletop to transfer over the plates of steaming food and big mugs of coffee. Tori smiled at her. "Thanks, Lindsay."

"No problem. Flag me down if you need anything else."

"We won't need anything else," Jericho replied with a quick grin before switching his gaze to the other side of the booth.

Again, Tori felt pinned by the intensity that burned there. After this many years of living, she'd have thought some of his intensity would have lessened, but not so much.

To cover her uneasiness, she picked up her coffee and let the cup hide her face as she took a deep draught. Ah, caffeine. It wouldn't help at all in settling her jangling nerves, but she loved the stuff, so who cared? "So...Mason and Celia."

"Yeah." He picked up the fork he'd been playing with when she came in and applied himself to his food with gusto. "Those two aren't going to make this easy. The last year of failed attempts is just going to make it harder to get them to break down and actually trust each other."

"Yeah, trust. It's a fickle thing." If there was a bite of irony to her voice, she didn't bother to cover it. She'd trusted him, and he'd betrayed her. Discussing how to help him make a woman trust anyone was like twisting the knife that had been parked squarely between her shoulder blades for over a hundred years. Not that she was bitter. Much.

His gaze cut to her, so she busied herself with her own dinner. He took a sip of his coffee, and she could feel his gaze on her, *willing* her to look at him, to make that connection, but she refused to give him what he wanted. They had a job to do. The personal shit between them could stay good and buried for all she cared. She was *never* going there again with him. His fingers tapped a light tattoo on the table. "We have to make this work. The last angel may have failed these people, but I'm not going to."

"Neither am I." She looked at him, her eyes narrowed. "I have never failed a client before and I don't intend to start now."

What they didn't say was that neither of them knew what happened if an angel failed. They were just...gone, replaced. Where they went was something no Guardian knew. Tori didn't guess anyone who'd failed got a promotion, but she didn't want to find out if the other option was a downward spiral to the hot spot. Some mysteries she'd learned not to wonder about. It was safer that way.

A pensive frown drew Jericho's brows together. "I had one assignment that didn't pan out."

"I don't even want to imagine what that means." A sick feeling hollowed out the pit of her belly. She told herself the feeling stemmed from the notion of going through that herself rather than the thought of Jericho coming so close to disappearing the way the angel he'd replaced here had been.

He sighed, shaking his head. He swallowed audibly, his voice hoarse. "The soul mate committed suicide. I had to hand my client over to a grief angel."

"Damn." *I'm sorry.* The words hovered on the tip of her tongue, but she bit them back. Offering sympathy, reaching out, would only make this situation worse for everyone concerned. Her heart twisted at the very idea of passing off a client that way, of having them hurt like that on her watch. For better or for worse, she came to care about all her people. In that, she knew she was lucky in her job. She got to help people find love—how the Guardians who dealt with ugly emotions like despair, depression, loss and suicide made it through the day was beyond her.

A shudder went through her. She was happy to keep her job, thanks so much. Failure was not an option. Mason and Celia were *going* to fall in love and they were *going* to be happy, even if she had to hog-tie their stubborn asses together for eternity. She stabbed her fork viciously into an innocent piece of broccoli.

"I don't know what you're thinking, but I know I don't like the look on your face." Lazy amusement curled through Jericho's voice, and he settled back against the smooth wood of the booth.

She tucked a stray lock of hair behind her ear, wrinkling

her nose. "Just thinking we may have to hog-tie our clients together or something to make this work."

"You always did have a fondness for being tied up." The amusement was still in his deep tone, but laced with rough desire, with hot memories she'd tried to scrub from her mind long ago.

How he'd snuck into her brother's encampment, bound her and gagged her, stealing her away in the middle of the night to hold as a hostage. How he'd removed the gag when he'd gotten her back to his camp, and she'd challenged him, hurled every insult she'd ever heard at him, cursing him in four different languages. How she'd still been bound when he'd kissed her, stroked her, made love to her the first time. How she'd moaned and sobbed and begged him for more.

Her nipples hardened and wetness slicked her sex as the erotic parade marched behind her eyes. Goose bumps rippled down her skin, and her blood rushed hot through her veins. She barely managed to swallow the bite of food in her mouth without choking. Pain and lust twisted like wild things inside her, shredding her until she wanted to howl with the awfulness of it. *Please, God, make it stop. Please.* She couldn't bear this. Not now. Not again. Not with him.

"No response, huh? Tori." He said the nickname slowly, as though savoring the taste of it on his tongue. "I like that. It suits you, darlin'."

"Don't call me that. I'm not your darling. I never was." She could have bitten her tongue off trying to snap her mouth shut. Too late. The words were out there, falling like heavy stones between them. She should have ignored his goading, shouldn't have mentioned the past at all, shouldn't even have acknowledged they had one. The very last thing she wanted was to rehash old times with him. The past was, by very definition, done and over with. It should stay that way.

His silver eyes zeroed in on her, made her want to squirm

in discomfort. A flash of what almost looked like hurt flickered in his gaze. She repressed a snort. Right. She'd have to matter to him to hurt his feelings, and she knew she never had.

That was how they'd ended up in this mess. In life, they'd been soul mates, destined for one another, even though they were wary and untrusting, on opposite sides of a war. Then she'd risked everything to warn him about a surprise raid Enrique had planned...only to find her beloved in bed with another woman.

A stray shot fired during the raid had taken her life, but she'd already been shattered beyond repair.

She hadn't known it then, but their own Guardians had failed them, and when Tori and Jericho had died because of that failure, they'd been recruited to replace their angels. That was how it worked. Failure meant another angel replaced you. Failure resulting in the death of a client meant the *client* replaced you. It was just Tori and Jericho's misfortune that *both* of them had died that day. And it was just Tori's luck that a man she never wanted to see again, a man who should have croaked at a ripe old age before the turn of the *last* century, had followed her into unwilling immortality.

Fuck.

Chapter Three

Tori grabbed her bag, tossed more than enough cash to cover their meal onto the table, shot out of her seat, and ran like hell. She couldn't do this. She *could not* do this.

He caught her on the street, of course. Jericho had never been one to let anything go. His fingers wrapped tight around her upper arm, pulling her to a stop and forcing her to face him. She kept her gaze pinned to his chest, grating out as few words as possible. "I need to go home."

She felt his gaze move over her, studying her—her face, her eyes, her breasts beneath the serviceable top she wore, her white-knuckled hold on the handle of her purse. "Fine. I'll walk you."

Shifting his inexorable grip, he steered her toward the small bed and breakfast inn she owned—or, at least, the angelic *woo-woo* of her cover identity meant people *thought* she owned it and *had* owned it for years and years. Thankfully, it was close to the town square, which the diner faced. They didn't have far to go. Still, she was painfully aware of his hand on her skin as they walked through the square. She hated herself for being unable to squelch her reaction. She wanted to run screaming, she wanted to tackle him to the ground and do filthy things to his body. She wanted to beat him to a pulp for hurting her and ruining her one chance at happiness. She did none of those things—the town gossip didn't make gossip for other people to spread around.

His hand on her elbow would look like nothing more than polite and solicitous assistance to an elderly lady, but the rough calluses on his fingertips rubbed in slow circles against her arm. Goose bumps raced over her limbs again and she shivered, her nipples tightening to painful points. She hadn't been this turned on in over a century. Not since the last time he'd touched her.

She turned her head to meet his gaze squarely, unflinching. "While we walk, let's discuss Mason and Celia. Then I'd like us to have as little contact as possible until this is over."

Again, she felt him study her, but she refused to be discomfited by him. He faced forward. "We should definitely talk about the assignment."

"Okay. Good." Relief that he didn't push the subject of their interactions, past or future, made the air squeeze out of her lungs.

"You've done a great job of steering Mason in the right direction, but it's obvious to anyone—including Celia—he's just looking to score. And get rid of what has to be a serious case of blue balls."

She choked, and a laugh exploded out of her. Wrapping her arm around herself, she tried to hold in the shrieks of laughter and not drop her purse. Hilarity made her voice shake. "I cannot *believe* you said that."

A rich chuckle answered her, and she watched the lines crinkle around his eyes as his white teeth flashed in a wide smile. "The truth hurts."

"Much like blue balls."

His broad shoulder lifted in a casual shrug. "It's hard on a guy."

"So I've heard." She snorted on another chuckle. "I'll take your word on it."

"They both have trust issues. They're wary. It's understandable, given their pasts." His dark brows drew together, his focus turning inward for a moment. Then he sighed and his lips quirked in a small grin. "Which is pretty much the same old story for what we do."

God, she loved his smile. She always had. He was freer with it now than he had been, which was good for him, and bad for her control. She'd always been a sucker for a man who could make her laugh. She slammed the brakes on that alarming and dangerous line of thought.

Jericho's breath caught. She shot a sharp glance at him in time to see him jerk his chin aside to stare at a tree as they passed another couple. She arched her eyebrows, but immediately recognized the chief of police and his wife, Aubrey. She smiled and nodded as they walked by, but the two were absorbed in each other and barely spared her a glance before they disappeared around a bend in the path.

"Your most recent conquest. Nicely done, by the way." Her eyebrows lifted higher. "You're in a different disguise, Jericho. They won't recognize you."

He grunted. "It's the eyes. No matter how many faces I wear, I've never gotten the eyes to change color."

"And it's a distinctive color. That is a problem."

"Not usually." He shrugged. "I move around with my assignments, so I'm not in one place long enough for anyone to notice."

True enough. Travel was the name of their game. "But you finished up with them, and there was a local project that fell in your lap."

"Something like that." Suddenly his eyes narrowed, flattening to a cold pewter. "You *knew* I was in town and you avoided me."

Damn. Caught. She hurried her steps, heaving a sigh of intense relief as the inn came into view. She kept her voice light, her tone dismissive. "I gave you a hand. Not that the chief needed any urging, but when he asked about Aubrey's dating habits, I filled him in, encouraged him a little. I *am* the town gossip, you know. Information sharing is what I do. I *also* used the dachshund I was dog sitting for a friend to trip her up and get her carried into his house for their first date. You're welcome."

"You avoided me." The words shot from his mouth like bullets, and she felt his muscular body tense. He dragged her to a stop in front of the B&B.

"I had my own assignment to deal with. There was no need to interact with you, no need to draw attention to ourselves." She set her jaw at a stubborn angle, daring him to refute her. His gaze heated with the challenge, and she almost groaned. Challenging Jericho was a mistake and she knew it. That was how she'd ended up flat on her back the night they'd met.

"Yes, there's no need to draw attention to ourselves. We shouldn't make a scene." His hand lifted, and he stroked a single fingertip across her cheekbone, trailed it to her jaw, and down her throat, where she knew he could feel her pulse pounding. His movements were slow, giving her the chance to pull away. She didn't. God, she craved him. She always had, and it stabbed at her heart to realize she always would.

She swayed toward him, her brain short-circuiting as an image of them in the privacy of her bedroom, in her bed, formed and refused to leave.

"It's not working, acting as if this is about our job. I want you too much to pretend I haven't been hard since the moment you walked into the restaurant tonight. You're still the most beautiful woman I've ever seen." His voice dropped to a low, silken purr that stroked over her nerves, exciting her, soothing her.

Her eyes closed as his words washed over her, undermining all of her righteous bitterness. Whether she liked it or not, she reacted to this man. No one could make her angrier, faster. No one could make her hornier, faster. This many months of celibacy only made it that much harder to resist the magnetic pull he had on her by just standing there and *breathing*. When he said things like that to her, used that tone of voice, it made fire flood her.

Swallowing, she glanced away and squeezed her thighs together to quell the ache between them. It was a wasted effort. "We're in public, Jericho. Don't forget when people look at us, they see an old lady and a gay man."

"Then let's go somewhere private because within the next five minutes you're going to be under me, whether we're in public or not." That stroking finger moved over her lips before curving under her chin and forcing her to meet his gaze, the steely, relentless determination that shone there. "I want you stripped and spread for me. I want my tongue in your mouth while you scream and sigh and moan. I want your nails digging into my back when I slide into that tight, wet little pussy of yours. I want to fuck you until neither of us can stand. And then I'm really going to get started on you."

She wanted that. All of that. So much that every other thought fled, her hormones rioted, her body overruling her mind.

They made it to the small guesthouse behind the inn that she used for her home before he had his hands all over her, but it was a close call. The door hadn't even swung shut before his mouth covered hers and his tongue thrust between her lips.

A moan ripped from her throat. He tasted the same—like honey and hot, wicked man. Like heaven on earth. Like Jericho. She twisted her fingers in his silky hair, holding him in place while she tangled her tongue with his. Her body burned, ached with emptiness, wetness flooding her core until she thought she might cry if he didn't fill her soon. She rocked herself against him in shameless abandon, her nails digging into his scalp as she sought to communicate her need. He groaned, but didn't slow down.

His palms slid over her back, one dipping down to cup her backside and lift her body into his. The rigid length of his cock rubbed against the juncture of her thighs. A low, choking cry issued from her throat, and she rose on tiptoe, wrapped one leg around his hip, and tried to ride his erection through both their pants. God, she craved him as much as she ever had. More. She ground herself against him in a desperate search for orgasm.

He made a rough, guttural noise, both hands on her ass, lifting her off her feet so she could twine her legs around his lean waist. Stumbling forward, he pressed her back to the wall and rolled his hips against hers, rubbing his cock right where she needed it. Stars burst behind her closed eyelids, pleasure swamping her in a rush. They still had all their clothes on and she was a heartbeat away from shattering.

She arched helplessly in his arms, her mouth ripping free of his as she writhed against him. "I'm so close, Jericho."

"Not yet, Tori. Not yet." He tugged at her legs, disentangling himself from her grip. She moaned a protest, her nails digging into his shoulders. His voice was a deep rasp in her ear, his accent thickening with his lust. "I want to be inside you when you come for me, darlin'. I want to feel it."

A sob ripped from her throat, and she clutched at him, her head rolling on the wall. Lust slammed into her in waves that threatened to drown her. "Hurry."

His hands were busy on the fly of her slacks, wrenching open the zipper and shoving them and her panties down her legs. He lifted her out of her loafers and braced her against the wall again. Her legs automatically wrapped around his hips as she tried to keep her balance, but there was no balance to be had with Jericho. There never had been.

"I can't wait." His words were little more than a breath of

air against her lips before he claimed her mouth again. The smooth, hot head of his cock nudged against her slick folds. She had no idea when he'd unfastened his own pants, but she didn't have time to wonder as he slammed deep with one hard thrust. Her back bowed in reflex to the sudden invasion, the thickness of him painful after so many months of celibacy. But even the pain became a slicing, white-hot blade of pleasure. She screamed for him then, just as he'd wanted, the sound high, thin and wild, smothered by his mouth.

He pounded into her, his movements fast and rough and so damn exciting she knew she'd come in minutes, seconds. A sob caught in her throat at losing this connection so soon, emotion she didn't want to feel ripping at her control. His fingers bit into her ass as he hitched her higher against the wall, changed the angle of his penetration, made it even better for her. He hit her G-spot with every thrust, and his tongue still moved boldly in her mouth, his honeyed flavor assaulting her, his masculine scent filling her tortured lungs with every gasping breath.

He took every part of her and claimed it for himself.

One hand slipped inward, the fingers circling the tight bud of her anus. She moaned, shuddered, her heart hammering at the thought of him touching her there, taking her there. A single fingertip pressed inward, and she tore her mouth away from his. "Yes! Oh, *yes*. Jericho!"

He just chuckled, the sound dark and smoky, and worked his finger deep into her ass. His cock pistoning in and out of her pussy, his finger massaging the tight ring of her anus, the feel and taste of him after so long, stripped what was left of her control. Her body bowed hard, her head falling back against the wall. She exploded in one unstoppable rush. Her sex convulsed around him, her muscles clenching, milking him until her mouth opened in a silent scream.

A hoarse, guttural groan jerked from him as orgasm gripped him. He shoved into her once, twice, three more times before his fluids erupted inside her. It was enough to push her over the edge again, her pussy fisting tight as helpless shivers wracked her body.

"Tori," he breathed, the word almost a prayer. Burying his face in the curve of her neck, he licked her, kissed her sensitized flesh.

Closing her eyes, she swallowed back the unwanted, unwarranted tears. Her mind refused to work, her thoughts drifting. She knew she should move, should push him away, but her muscles were as unresponsive as her brain, so she just stayed where she was, panting for breath, waiting for her racing heartbeat to slow. Waiting for reality to come roaring back to bitch-slap her.

They both groaned when his cock began to length and harden inside her again, expanding to stretch her from deep inside. He straightened away from the wall, wrapped his arms tight around her, and walked unsteadily through the open bedroom door. Cradling her close, he lowered them both to the cool, smooth quilt, and sipped soft kisses from her lips as he went.

He leaned back just enough to peel her shirt off, unsnap her bra and fling the soft cotton garments away. His big hands cupped her breasts, lifting them for his mouth. Her breath tangled in her throat as anticipation sliced through her. God, but she wanted his mouth on her. She arched her back in offering. He grinned, flicking his tongue out to wet each tight nipple. "I have to say, women's underwear is a hell of a lot easier to get rid of now than it was back then."

Her laugh sounded more like a needy whimper. "You're telling me. You never had to *wear* a damn corset."

"Thank God for that." And then he took her nipple in his mouth to suckle, and a deep moan burst from her. Sheer pleasure arced from her breast to her loins, and her pussy clenched hard around his cock. He groaned, setting his teeth

94

into her nipple in response. She squealed, a fresh tide of wetness flooding her sex. Her hands lifted to his shoulders, her nails digging in deep, raking down his flesh. He grunted, swirling his tongue around and around her nipple before he shoved it hard against the roof of his mouth.

A low cry was the only articulation she could give to the heat, the need, the desperation exploding within her. Her thighs cinched on his waist as she tried to pull him deeper, squeezing him with her inner muscles, milking him until he shuddered and finally, *finally* began moving inside her. Her hips undulated beneath him, their harsh breathing, soft groans and slapping flesh the only sounds in the room. The scents of sweat and sex perfumed the air, a drugging aphrodisiac that made her burn.

She closed her eyes to savor how amazing it felt to have him over her and in her again, his heavy weight pressing her into a soft bed, his wide cock making her body work to accommodate him. It was pleasure and it was pain and it was exactly what she craved. An addict getting her fix after so many sober years on the bandwagon. He ground his hips against her clit, and she sobbed, digging her heels into the backs of his muscular thighs.

"Look at me, Tori," he demanded. "I want to watch you come."

She obeyed and was snared by his silver gaze. She had no idea what he saw in her face, but triumph and possession and a myriad of other emotions she couldn't name blazed across his expression. Her movement faltered, some belated caution rising to the surface of her consciousness.

"Nuh-uh. None of that." His eyes narrowed, and his fingers slid between them to flick over her clit again and again until she strained upward and danced on the ragged edge of orgasm. Still, she couldn't look away from him. The dark flush running under his tanned skin, the kiss-swollen lips, the gleam of desperate hunger in his gaze. It was the desperation that captivated her. Jericho had never worn such a look before, not once. Lust, fury, greed—yes. Soul-deep desperation—no.

She wanted it to mean something, wanted it so badly, it shamed her, made tears well in her eyes and streak unchecked down her cheeks. His palms rose to frame her face, and he nuzzled and licked her tears away. When he kissed her, she tasted the salty moisture on his lips. The gentle reverence of the kiss was such a wild contrast to the roughness of his thrusting cock that it made her sob into his mouth, made her hotter and wetter, her inner flesh clinging to him. He angled his hips, slamming deeper, harder and it sent her flying.

Her pussy clenched in rhythmic spasms that went on forever, dragged her under until she had no sense of time or space. There was only Jericho's hands and mouth and muscular body driving her beyond sanity and into pure sensation. Every heavy thrust sent another orgasm screaming through her, made her throb around him. Tingles broke down her arms and legs, shivers she couldn't control wracking her.

"Tori, I—" His words broke off in a low groan as she came again, her thighs tightening on his flanks, her pussy wringing his cock. He shuddered and jetted deep inside her, a muscle in his jaw ticking as he gritted his teeth. "Oh, God, *Vitoria*. My Tori."

He sank down on her, his heavy weight crushing her into the mattress. Sweat sealed their bodies together, and she could barely drag air into her overtaxed lungs. Her muscles went slowly limp, still shaking in the aftermath. Her legs fell to the quilt, and she sighed. He grunted, heaving himself to the side so she could breathe again. He hooked an arm around her hips and dragged her back against him. Within minutes, his breathing leveled out into that of deep slumber. She stared at the ceiling, her thoughts hazy, and she felt hollowed out by what had happened, what she'd never thought would happen again.

What *should never* have happened again. Reality returned in an awful rush, her gut clenching as nausea burned away the lingering tendrils of contentment that wound through her. Jesus, what had she *done*? Was she insane? Did she have some kind of crazy need to commit emotional suicide?

Tears burned in her eyes as she turned away from him, curled into herself, and clamped a hand over her mouth to stifle a harsh sob. It caught in her throat, threatening to strangle her. What the hell was *wrong* with her? She'd just rolled right over and spread her legs for him, like nothing bad had ever happened between them, like he'd never betrayed her. He was her soul mate, and she had no defenses against him. With him, she was so fucking weak. Pathetic. Needy. A huge failure. Just as she'd always been.

No wonder he'd turned to another woman.

Chapter Four

He was already inside her when she woke up, the first rays of dawn flickering through her window. She arched, her body already hot and slick and more than ready for whatever he wanted. His arms were wrapped tight around her torso, her back to his front, and he rocked against her in infinitesimal strokes that only aroused her more.

"Good morning." His sleep-roughened voice slid over her nerves like velvet. His big palm slipped down to spread across her lower belly, pressing her deeper into his thrusts. "Did you sleep well?"

"*Mmm...*" A more articulate answer was beyond her. No, she hadn't slept well, but at the moment, she didn't care. All she wanted was for him to fuck her harder, faster, until the only thing she could think about was the mindless drive to orgasm. A deep pang passed through her as she realized she wouldn't—*couldn't*—tell him to stop. She wanted him too badly. She clenched her jaw tight as her need to protect herself warred briefly with her need for his touch, for connection, for pleasure. Swallowing back a hopeless, helpless moan, she gave in to the ecstasy he offered. *Later* was soon enough to kick her own ass for her weakness, her stupidity, her failure. Her hand wrapped around his imprisoning forearm, her nails digging in as she sought the freedom to move.

Ignoring her wordless demand, he flicked his tongue over the sensitive tendon that connected her neck and shoulder. She shivered, her nipples tightening in reflex. He noticed—of course he noticed, Jericho had never missed the merest hint of response from her—and his other palm moved to fondle her breasts, his fingertips whispering over her flesh. Just the way she liked it. How had he remembered after all this time? She gasped, her head falling back on his shoulder, her torso bowing outward as she struggled against his superior strength.

It was almost as good as when he tied her down to sex her up.

Just the thought was enough to fan the flames of her excitement, to make her wetter.

As if he'd read her mind, a chuckle vibrated through his broad chest. "Not this time, darlin', but soon I'm going to tie you to this bed. That fancy wrought-iron headboard will do just fine for what I have in mind."

Oh, God, it would. She tried not to imagine it, and failed. Molten lava pumped through her veins, sped by her racing heart. Jericho bit her neck lightly and the unexpected sting made her cry out. She rocked her hips back, trying to take him deeper, to push him into going faster. Reaching back, she clamped a hand on the muscular globe of his ass, her nails gouging deep. "*Now*, Jericho."

"*Yes*," he gritted between clenched teeth. His hips bucked, and finally he gave her the hard penetration she craved.

The smack of his skin against hers, the hard impact of his belly on her backside, echoed in her bedroom. The bedsprings squeaked underneath them, the antique bed frame creaked. Their low groans and soft cries added layer upon layer to the carnal symphony they played together. Sweat dampened her skin, and her muscles strained as she pushed herself harder. More. She wanted more. She wanted everything.

He slipped his fingers down between her legs, rubbing her clit in time with his strokes, letting his movements drive her harder against his fingertips to increase the already unbearable friction. She was wet, hot. Her pussy clenched once, and he made a rough sound of pure pleasure that turned her inside out, it was so good. The way his cock filled her was perfect. It always had been, it always would be. She blinked back the sting of tears and clutched his arm, held tight to the moment she was in.

Shudders began building deep inside her, orgasm rising high and hot to claim her. She held it off, wanting to stay right here where everything felt good and right and perfect. Clenching her inner muscles did nothing to aid her, and a sob of despair slid from her. Too soon. It was ending far too soon.

"Shh, shh, darlin'." His voice soothed and aroused, stroked over her as effectively as a caress. His free hand lifted to toy with her breasts, to pluck and twist her nipples until she bit her lip against another sob. "Trust me—I'll give you what you need."

No, he wouldn't. She knew that, knew it all the way down to her soul, and it ripped at her, an agonizing pain that made her scream. Then he lunged deep within her, deeper than he'd been before, and the scream changed as she shattered. Her body exploded with an ecstasy that consumed every piece of her. She convulsed in his arms, her pussy flexing on his cock in rhythmic waves that dragged him down into the whirlpool with her.

"Tori, Tori, *Tori.*" His come flooded her, and they rocked together, savoring every single moment of the fiery pleasure they generated together.

She sighed and closed her eyes. Agony and ecstasy pulsed through her in equal measures that could only be defined by one whispered word—"Jericho."

There was nothing else to say.

The morning was wonderful.

Jericho dragged her out of bed after their pre-dawn mattress romp and coaxed her into getting coffee from the best shop in town, Bean There, Done That. The little café was owned by his last client, Aubrey, so Tori went in to buy the liquid ambrosia alone, but then they meandered through the park and down a few quiet side streets—not talking...just *being*. It was nice. She liked it way too much and it sent a sick little twist through her stomach. She swallowed the mouthful of latte she had before she choked on it.

His eyes were pure mercury when he glanced down at her. "My apartment is just over there." He tilted his head to indicate a pretty three-story converted Victorian across the street from where they were standing. "We still have hours before we need to be at work. Let me make you breakfast."

That wasn't all he wanted to make.

Bleakness flooded her soul. She couldn't tell him no. She didn't even want to. Even if it was for her own good. "Okay."

She followed him into the building and up the stairs, knowing it was a mistake, knowing she was going to get hurt, knowing that the only way to protect herself was to set the ground rules. As far as he'd ever know, she felt the same way he did, the same way he had felt from their first meeting. This was just sex, a good lay, a great fuck. There was no *love*making, just hot, wild, lusty sex. If they didn't drag her battered heart into the equation, if they focused on the physical, and on the present, she might survive this.

Then again, it wasn't as if she could *die* again, was it? She'd already given everything she had. Body, heart, soul, *life*. Everything. And still she had failed.

Sucking in a deep breath, she squared her shoulders and stepped into his apartment. She wouldn't fail again. She was stronger than she had been, and she had a hell of a lot more experience. A hundred plus years on Earth would do that to a person. She wasn't the naïve, sheltered girl she had been. She could survive this. She could survive Jericho, she could survive losing this connection again, she could and *would* do her job and walk away. She'd done it before, and while things were more complicated this time, it didn't mean she couldn't do it again.

Until it was time to leave, she was going to indulge herself in the sexiest man she'd ever known. She knew herself well enough to know she had no choice, so she wasn't going to fight it. The past was beyond her control, but the present and the future were hers to shape. Even angels had some free will, and she was going to exercise it.

Jericho shut the door and flipped the lock. The place was homier than she'd expected. The furnishings were comfortable and a little worn around the edges, heavy dark wood that was a direct contrast to the light beach house wicker at her cottage. It was very much Jericho, and nothing like the overtly gay man he was playing for this assignment. His inner sanctum. She slid her hands in her pockets and chuckled. They turned to each other, and she opened her mouth to tease him about it when he cupped her face between his big palms. The expression he wore was serious, but light glinted in his eyes. Her breath tangled in her throat, and her heart skipped a beat. She swallowed, tried to grin and break the sudden tension of the moment. He stroked a thumb over her lower lip, and her smile died before it fully formed.

Bending forward, he brushed his mouth over hers. The kiss was infinitely tender, underscored by the passion that always blazed between them. She hummed in her throat and let herself melt against him. Her breasts flattened against the wall of muscle that made up his broad chest. Flicking her tongue out to lick his lips, she parted them and found her way inside his mouth, reveling in the taste of him. Sweet, rich honey. She moaned, wriggling to get closer, twining her fingers in the rough silk of his hair.

Rising on tiptoe, she fitted her sex against his cock, writhing against him like a cat in heat, rubbing her breasts against his chest to stimulate her nipples. Her heart pumped her blood wild and fast through her veins, the scent of him, the flavor of him, the sheer size and heat of him made her pussy go slick, the folds plumping as her body readied itself for sex. Her fingers tightened in his hair, tugging as her need spiked. She bit his lower lip, sucking it between her teeth.

He groaned and pulled away, searched her face, gave a little smile, and then planted a few more soft, warm kisses on her lips. "I told myself I was going to *talk* to you, not dive on you the moment the door shut, but you just have to look at me and my control goes haywire." He trailed his fingertips across her jaw. "We need to talk. About us. What we're doing, where we're going. And especially where we've been. I have a lot—"

"No." She jerked back, stepping outside of his arm's reach, moving away until her legs pressed against his big dining room table. It hurt to deny herself contact with him, but she had some self-preservation left. Pulling in a deep breath to calm her racing heartbeat, she forced herself to recall the gut-wrenching moment when she'd walked into a saloon to find him sharing a bed with a whore. Sure, they'd argued, he'd dumped her back off in her brother's camp, but really? That was all his *soul mate* had meant to him? A convenient lay? Less than a day after they'd parted, and he'd *paid* to fuck another woman. The memory was a splash of cold water on her overheating hormones, a stab of utter agony to her heart. She narrowed her eyes at him, her shaking fists clenched at her sides. "You want this thing between us, that's fine, but the deal is we do not talk about the past. At all. Ever. It didn't happen."

"It did happen." Now it was his turn to narrow his eyes, and she saw rage burn in his gaze, but he banked the emotion, and his voice was almost even when he spoke. "Just trust me for once and *listen* to what—"

"*No.*" She shook her head and folded her arms protectively over her chest. "Not just no, but *hell no.* You want to keep getting hot and heavy with me while we're working together on this assignment, then we don't talk about anything that went on before now. That's over. We already failed the test. It doesn't matter anymore." She met his eyes, refusing to back down. She'd already had to piece together a broken heart once before, and she doubted it could stand a second round. "That's the deal. Take it or leave it."

"I'll take it." He jerked her against him, and the fury he no longer tried to control made his eyes an incandescent silver. "Let's start now."

His mouth slammed down over hers, his tongue thrusting into her mouth to demand a response from her. She gave it, matching his demands with her own. They fought for control of the kiss, biting, sucking and nipping at each other until their skin was hot to the touch, burning up. Their breathing was nothing but harsh rasps, and they groaned into each other's mouth. She tasted blood, but didn't know if it was his or hers. It didn't matter, the copper tang of it drove her excitement to a primitive, carnal place.

They came together with the same speed and urgency of the night before, but instead of desperation, this was a furious claiming. All the building anger, pain and desire they couldn't deny exploded between them. She grabbed the front of his shirt and ripped it open, the buttons scattering in every direction. Then her hands were on his chest, thumbing his flat little nipples. He groaned, broke the kiss and wrenched her shirt over her head. Her bra shredded under the same treatment, but his mouth was on her breasts, sucking her hard, making her back bow as pleasure speared straight to her pussy. Her inner walls clenched on nothingness, and she shuddered.

He bit her nipple, batted it with his tongue and bit her again. She gritted her teeth on a scream. Her fingers fisted in his hair, twisting until he grunted at the pain. "Fuck me, Jericho."

"Whatever you want, *darlin'*." The words were harsh with sarcasm, strained with unsated lust.

Grabbing her shoulders, he spun her around and forced her to bend over the table. His hands jerked open her pants and shoved them and her panties down her legs. She kicked them aside, her heart pounding as she heard the clink of his belt buckle, the rasp of his zipper, and then he crowded between her thighs. His cock was like a thick, hot pipe pressing against her buttocks, sliding into the crevice. His arms wrapped around her torso, one hand moving down to shove into her sex. She bucked against him, but it did nothing to dislodge him. She was caught, trapped, and it made the flames licking through her even hotter.

Three big fingers filled her pussy, stretching her. He didn't give her time to adjust, just thrust high and hard into her soaking channel. This time, there was no holding back her scream. It was too much, and not nearly enough. He worked her until she thought she'd faint, her wetness growing with every plunge of his fingers inside her. He pulled from her abruptly, making her crying out at the loss. Using her own moisture, he slid those same fingers one by one into her backside. Shudders wracked her body, and she whimpered when his other hand took the place of the first, filling her pussy. It was more than she could bear. She came, screaming. Her sex milked his fingers, tingles exploding over her skin as she rocked herself between his hands.

Fire flashed in her blood, sweat slid down her temples, and all she could do was let her head fall back as she moaned. "Jericho. My Jericho."

"Yes," he groaned, the sound tormented pleasure. "God, *yes.*"

His fingers jerked from her ass, and she felt him position his cock at the entrance of her anus. Oh. *Jesus.* A whimper fell from her throat, and his thick cock pressed her wider than his

105

hand had. The tight ring of her anus bore down on him, and she forced her shaking muscles to relax, to accept the hot invasion. Anticipation pumped her blood even faster through her veins, a sizzle of ecstasy arcing through her overloaded system. He worked his cock deeper and deeper. She fell forward on her palms, bracing herself on the smooth wood table so she could move with him, take all of him. He thrust slowly at first, but picked up speed and force until his taut belly spanked against the softer curve of her buttocks.

The heel of his palm rotated against her clit, and her breath caught in shock. His hand worked her pussy to the same rhythm as his cock in her ass. His fingertips rubbed the thin layer of flesh between her two channels, stimulating her to a point she'd never reached before. Her nails raked across the tabletop, her back bowing as he fucked her hard and rough. Taking her. Possessing her. His palm slapped against her clit with each movement of his hand, his pelvis grinding into her ass. A wave of ecstasy hit her, almost taking her over the edge. Almost. God, she was so damn *close*. A few more strokes of that big cock in her anus, a couple of flicks of those clever fingers and she would break. He paused for just a moment, a fraction of a second, but it was enough to make her cry out in desperate longing. He couldn't stop now. She'd throttle him if he tried.

Jericho's deep rumble reverberated in her ear, the tone silky, dangerous. "Deny it all you want, darlin', but we belong to each other. *You belong to me.*" His hot breath washed over her skin, making goose flesh break down her limbs. His thrusts became wilder, fiercer. "I don't have to talk about the past for you to know you're mine, Tori. *Mine.* You always have been, you always will be. You'll never be free of me, you'll never get the feel of me off your skin, the taste of me out of your mouth. You. Are. Mine. My soul mate. Just plain old fucking *mine.*"

"I hate you!"

He laughed at her, bit the back of her shoulder, licked the

stinging flesh until she panted. "No, you don't. You only wish you could."

He was right, damn him.

Those wicked fingers rubbed her G-spot, and he shoved his cock deep in her ass, deeper than he'd ever been before and she was lost. She shattered, pushed beyond her endurance. Her inner muscles clenched around his fingers, his cock, and her entire body undulated against him in wanton abandon. Her skin felt too hot and too tight to hold in the ecstasy roiling through her, splintering her into a million unrecognizable pieces.

The last thing she heard before reality dissolved around her was his growl of "*Mine.*"

Her eyes rolled back, and she collapsed forward. He caught her, cradled her against his chest, brushed her sweat-dampened hair away from her face, kissed her temple. He whispered something against her skin, but she didn't hear it. Consciousness slipped away, and she welcomed the sweet nothingness of oblivion.

Chapter Five

Tori dreamed about her last day as a human every night that week, her subconscious's constant reminder to keep her guard up around Jericho, to not get too close, to never repeat her past mistakes. Because she might help other people fall in love, but her final hours as a human proved beyond a shadow of a doubt that she was a failure in the love department—always had been, always would be.

She just wished the details had grown fuzzier with time, but they hadn't. The nightmare always started in the same place. She and Jericho arguing. Again. She'd wanted to see Enrique, to assure her brother that she was all right. She'd hated that she knew he'd be worried, and she'd been certain if she explained to him how she felt about Jericho, that he'd understand, that he'd give them his blessing. Jericho didn't want to release her as his prisoner, but her insistence had finally paid off and he'd returned her to her brother—or maybe he'd just gotten sick of listening to her, and his sexual toy had been less fun to play with. Her reputation had already been tattered beyond repair, so the damage to her brother's honor had been done.

The reasons didn't matter, in the end. All that mattered was that things hadn't gone the way she'd planned. She'd been such a naïve little idiot. Enrique hadn't understood—he'd refused to let her go back to a man who'd stolen her virtue. Nothing she said would make him believe she loved Jericho, that she didn't want to live without him.

Her mind was locked in the dream, wanting to change how it ended, kicking and screaming and railing at herself, but it always ended the same. She could only watch and wait and live through her own demise over and over again. It was like *Groundhog Day* on crack.

She'd managed to escape Enrique's guards during the chaos of preparations for a surprise raid, and ridden her horse into the little backwater Texas town Jericho and his men occupied. Getting lost in the dark twice, terrified she wouldn't be able to warn Jericho in time, her memory tormented her with every moment of the horrifying panic of that ride. One of Jericho's men had reluctantly told her where to find him—the local saloon. The *brothel*. She hadn't wanted to believe, but she couldn't deny the truth that faced her—her brother had been right, Jericho had only used her to taunt an enemy, and she was a fool. She'd blurted out the information about Enrique's plans, that Jericho and his men were in danger, and then she'd staggered out, too broken, too numb to know or care where she should go next. She'd just gotten back on her horse and left. Jericho hadn't tried to stop her, hadn't come after her, hadn't cared that she'd been caught in the raid. He hadn't cared that she'd died trying to save his life. And he certainly hadn't had the decency to *live* and make her sacrifice worth something.

Every morning she jerked awake, back in her own bed, but sweat-soaked and shaking. Jericho was always there, reaching out to soothe her, and that soothing led to sex. Which meant her nerves were shot. Her senses were overloaded with both the remembered pain of Jericho and the overwhelming pleasure of being in his arms again.

It was enough to make her crazy. It sure as hell kept her a regular and loyal customer of Bean There, Done That. Caffeine was the only thing getting her through the days. She swallowed and offered Mason a smile when he noticed she'd stepped into line behind him. "Your Celia will be back from her convention tomorrow."

She'd often *accidentally* run into him at the coffee shop, so if it was a little more often than usual this week, no one wondered why. If she could get in just a little encouragement here and there, it wouldn't hurt. Keep him thinking about his soul mate, remind him he wanted her.

Mason grinned his pirate's grin, showing even white teeth. "She's not *my* Celia. Yet."

"Well, she's a fool to turn you down, young man." Tori threw in an extra little old lady creak to her voice and patted his brawny arm.

He laughed, his eyes dancing with real amusement. She got the impression he was bemused and a little touched that the kindly old town gossip took such an interest in his campaign to win Celia over. "Why, thank you, ma'am. I think so too."

Sweeping his arm in front of him in a roughly gallant gesture, he let her step up to the counter and order her coffee first. He really was a nice guy, if they could just get him and Celia on the right track. Tori sighed, her smile crumbling when she turned her back on him.

Even with the ugly nightmares, the days had whipped by, time racing when she wanted it to slow down. Dread settled like a cold, twisted knot in her belly. For better or for worse, this thing with Jericho would be over soon.

Somehow, her subconscious's less-than-subtle nightly memos weren't enough. She was more in love with him than she ever had been before, and it made her want to vomit. Maybe she should have been surprised at the depth of her reaction, but she wasn't. Soul mating was her business, and she knew from personal experience what happened when things went wrong. Maybe that was why failed soul mates became this kind of Guardian. Who better to understand the importance of their missions? Who better to appreciate the difficulty, the *agony,* of falling in love?

Jericho had kept to their deal. He hadn't brought up their

painful past, and Tori did her best to block out the nightmares and pretend it had never happened, to live in the now, to absorb the utter joy of being with a man crafted specifically for her.

It almost worked. When she was in his arms, she could almost forget. Almost.

As much as she loved every moment she spent with him, talking to him, being near him, a part of her would never belong to him, a piece of her heart and mind would never let her go all the way. And she was grateful. It would make it easier when they parted. She knew that, and still she ached. Ached for what was to come, and for what could never be.

She swayed on her feet, and Mason caught her elbow. "Whoa, Mrs. Chambers. You okay?"

His gaze had sharpened with both concern and professionalism. As a firefighter, he had medical training. Shit. She tried not to wince, straightened her shoulders, and offered the most genuine smile she could muster. "I'm just fine. Don't you worry."

Nodding easily, he didn't relinquish his grip on her arm. "Why don't I walk you back to the inn anyway? Just for my peace of mind."

It wasn't a request, and she knew it. Her grin was more genuine this time as amusement stole through her. A guardian angel couldn't get sick, couldn't get hurt, couldn't die. His anxiety was touching, and only made her more determined to get things right for him and his soul mate. She and Jericho may have screwed the pooch for themselves, but as Jericho had said, they wouldn't fail these people.

The trip to the bed and breakfast only took a few minutes, and she left Mason on the sidewalk to try to bury herself in the business of the inn. Cover story or not, she had to keep it running smoothly. It gave her something to think about besides

Jericho and their assignment, so she was grateful for the distraction. She checked the rooms, chatted with guests, served tea and cakes, then immersed herself in paperwork. A typical workday, and the routine of it after a year was soothing. Her night manager rousted her from the small office behind the check-in counter at just after seven that evening, shooing her toward the back door and her little cottage.

Jericho would be there soon. He'd made sure they spent every night together this week. Sometimes in her bed, sometimes in his. So, she waited, anticipation creating a lovely buzz in her system—or maybe it was just her brain buzzing from too much coffee and too little rest. She puttered around, put in a pan of lasagna for dinner, took a basket of clean laundry into her bedroom to fold and put away. The house was quiet, peaceful. It reminded her of the solitary life she led, and how lonely it could be. Banishing the unwanted thought, she forced her attention to the task at hand. She was hanging a dress in her small walk-in closet when Jericho arrived. She didn't hear him come in, she just became aware of him standing in her bedroom, watching her with that intent gaze of his.

"I took dinner out of the oven to cool. It smells great." He braced his shoulder against the doorjamb to her closet.

"Thanks."

Without trying, he dominated the space, his shoulders blocking the light streaming in from her bedroom. She reached overhead to jerk the chain attached to the overhead light. The naked bulb flooded the space with brightness, and she blinked to clear the sudden spots from her vision. Finished putting away the last of her laundry, she turned to exit. Jericho was still there, but he wasn't looking at her. Instead, he stroked a finger down a jumble of silk scarves she had dangling from one hanger. When he met her gaze, his expression was considering, but the tiny smile that twitched the corners of his lips was pure sin.

"These are pretty."

She swallowed, trying to generate some moisture in her suddenly parched throat. "I like them."

"I'm glad." His voice dropped to a low rumble that reached down deep inside her. "Take off your clothes."

"Jericho..."

"Things have been so good this week, haven't they? Better than ever, for me, anyway. But I want more from you. I've been dying to have you at my mercy, Tori. Let me. You know you like it, you want it. I want it." Some emotion she couldn't recognize flittered through his gaze, quickly masked behind a persuasive little grin. He plucked up a handful of the scarves, sliding them between his long fingers. She stared, mesmerized. "Let me please you, Vitoria."

She hadn't let him tie her up in the last week, deliberately. He'd hinted, but she'd always managed to distract him. It was too intimate, too trusting. But the effect of days on end with him, the sweetness of it, had drugged her. A slow, insidious contentment had wound through her. She closed her eyes, swallowed, her heart twisting in her chest.

"Please..." But she didn't know what she was asking for—for him to stop tempting her, for him to give her exactly what he'd offered.

The light in front of her shifted, and when she looked at him again, she saw he'd stepped back to allow her to pass him. She swayed until her breasts brushed his chest, and when she met his gaze, he groaned at whatever he saw there. Tossing the scarves across the foot of the bed, he reached for her, had them both naked before her brain could even fully acknowledge what she was about to let him do. Despite all her very good reasons, her resistance crumbled. It always did with him. This *thing* she had going with him now would be over soon, and she would never have this chance again. So, she'd take it. Her eyes were open, she knew what she was doing. She just hoped her heart survived.

He stretched her arms over her head, looping silky fabric around each of her wrists and then attaching them to the swirls of wrought iron that made up her headboard. She tested the bindings, tugging at them while he repeated the process with her ankles. The muscles in her thighs tensed in an automatic motion to protect herself from so much vulnerability, but she couldn't close her legs, couldn't move. A shudder ran through her when he flipped on the bright bedside lamp, framing her in a circle of light that made her feel even more exposed.

Excitement whipped through her, even though she reminded herself this was temporary insanity. He moved between her thighs, forcing her legs even wider. His cock was a hard arc that danced just under his navel, pre-come already rolling in slow beads down the long shaft. The sight made her belly clench and molten heat pumped through her veins. She waited for him to touch, to take, but instead he just stared down at her. When he spoke, his voice shook. "You are so damn beautiful."

She swallowed, made a smile quirk her lips. "You're not so bad yourself, cowboy."

It was nothing less than the truth. Jericho had a gorgeous body—the kind that made women pant, all broad shoulders and narrow hips, rippling abs and tight pecs. Plus, he was hung. She tried not to drool, but this was a fantasy come true. Bound, naked, and offered up like a buffet for his pleasure. With any other man, that might be a problem for her, but this was Jericho. She knew he'd make it good for her. In that, he'd never failed her.

He reached for her. His dark hair fell over his forehead as he leaned forward, his heavy-lidded gray eyes shining with naked desire. Her nipples tightened when his gaze touched them, and she strained against the silk scarves, wanting to get

114

closer to him. That she couldn't only made it better for her, made her *burn*. A fine tremor ran through his hands when he stroked over her collarbone, down to shape her breasts in his palms. Her breath caught as his callused hands stimulated her sensitive nipples. He lifted her breasts, kissed the soft, plumped curves. His touch was gentle, and far too slow to satisfy her. She was so ready when he took her nipple into his mouth and began to suckle that she screamed and jerked on the scarves. Tears blurred her vision and tingles flowed in rippling waves over every inch of her flesh. She was damp, flushed, ready for him to take her and there wasn't a damn thing she could do to hurry him up. God she loved this, loved *him*, loved the way he touched her, kissed her, pleased her. She gritted her teeth to suppress the urge to tell him. Giving him that much would destroy her, and she knew it. All she could do was take what he offered—sex—hot, sweaty and dirty.

The smooth, hard head of his cock brushed over the lips of her pussy. Need clawed at her, made her writhe in response. She arched herself for him, a silent offering, a demand, and he chuckled. The sound was nothing short of sinful, and it ratcheted up her anticipation even further. "I can't wait much longer, Jericho."

"Yes, you can. You will. And you'll like it." He moved down her body, his broad shoulders keeping her thighs spread wide, and his breath whispered over the moist folds of her swollen sex. "I promise."

She whimpered, tugging hard on her bindings, desperate for the wild, mindless pleasure only he had ever given her. The first stroke of his tongue on her pussy made her jolt, scream and twist. His lips closed over her clit and sucked. The breath exploded from her lungs and she couldn't drag in enough oxygen to plead, beg, and cry for more, for relief, for anything and everything he had to give her as long as he kept that wicked promise. Her muscles throbbed with the strain of pulling at the ties on her ankles and wrists, but she couldn't lie still. She craved him so much.

His rough, callused fingertips brushed up the insides of her thighs, raising goose bumps on her flesh and making her shiver. He teased the lips of her sex before easing two thick fingers into her slick channel. The rhythm he set for her was hard, punishing, his fingers and tongue working her until her eyes rolled back in her head. Her entire body shook, fire flowing through her in scorching waves. Her pussy spasmed, locking tight around those fingers. Then he twisted them, hooking his fingertips until they rubbed her in just the right place. A high wail broke from her throat as she convulsed in his arms. Still he pushed her, stroking her and sucking her wet flesh until the need rebuilt, until she was sobbing with the force of a second orgasm rocketing through her.

"*Jericho*. Jericho, please. I need...I can't...*please*."

"Oh, but I think we've already established that you *can*." He all but purred the words, his lips brushing against her clit as he spoke.

She licked her lips, trying to focus. "I want you inside me, Jericho."

"I want to be inside you," he whispered, his cool breath on her hot flesh making her pussy clench around his fingers. "I want to be deeper inside you than you've ever let anyone. Even me. I want you to trust me enough to let me in that deep."

The words sent an ominous shiver down her spine, and she knew he was talking about a lot more than trusting him during sex. It was more than she could give him. She closed her eyes, pulling at the silk around her wrists. She wished it was just the bindings that made her helpless in his embrace, but she knew it wasn't. *He* didn't need to know that though. She swallowed, moaned when his hand began thrusting again. "Jericho, please..."

He sighed, and she could feel his disappointment roll over her, and it hurt to upset him. She knew she shouldn't feel that way, but logic and emotion were two very different things. Rising on his elbows, he settled over her and slid his cock into her. It was so good she wanted to cry.

The hair on his chest rasped her nipples, and she couldn't help how she arched under him to increase the stimulation. He moved within her in tiny thrusts that drove her mad. She lifted her face for him to kiss, wanting his lips on her skin, but he just smiled down at her. His fingers stroked over her cheekbone, and the way he looked at her, so hot and sweet and tender... God, it was the look he used to use when she'd told herself he loved her. What a joke. And, in the end, the joke had been on her. She turned her head into her arm, unable to bear the memories that bombarded her, but she was tied down, so there was no escaping him, even if she wanted to. She shivered. What a horrible, awful mess.

"Don't look away from me, darlin'." He feathered a kiss over her jaw. "Be here with me."

Meeting that silver gaze that always saw too much, she waggled her bound wrists. "I'm not going anywhere."

His gaze searched her face for long moments before a look of stubborn determination molded his features. "That isn't what I meant, but it'll do. For now."

The slow strokes of his cock picked up speed, and she wished she could wrap her legs around his waist to lift herself into his thrusts. As if he'd read her mind, he angled his hips so he moved within her just right. It was so perfect it was painful, and something crumpled inside her. God, it was going to hurt to lose him again. She stared up at him, wanting to see his every expression, wanting to remember every detail. Wanting *something* to offset the ugly way things had ended the first time.

Squeezing her walls tight around him, she smiled when he groaned for her. She saw the moment his control snapped, felt

117

the shudder that wracked his big body. He plunged into her hard enough to make stars burst behind her eyes, and she gasped. He buried his face in her neck, but his rhythm didn't falter and his cock filled her again and again, his sharp hipbone slapping against her clit. Orgasm shimmered through her, building so high and fast, she had to bite back a scream.

His bellowing breath rushed against her throat. "No one else has ever done this to you before, have they, Tori?"

"Only you." As if she'd ever been able to let anyone take control of her pleasure this way. As if she'd ever put herself out there again after how monumental her failure had been the first time. She bucked beneath him, jerking at the silk ties. She wanted him to go even faster, to push her over that blissful edge.

"Only me." His voice was warm, possessive. Dangerous.

A warning sounded in her mind, distracting her from the drive to ecstasy. Her movements faltered.

His didn't.

If anything, he only made it worse, going faster and deeper, just the way she needed him to. He pounded into her, grinding against her clit, and sent her careening into ecstasy. Her sex pulsed around him, and she did scream then. His head lifted, and his gaze snared her. There was nothing but him, her whole world narrowed to this moment with this man, this fulfillment. Her pussy milked his cock, the contractions rippling deep within her, her orgasm going longer than she'd ever experienced before. He kept thrusting, kept dragging it out for her. She whimpered, writhing in her bindings, her skin so sensitized it was almost more than she could bear. "Come with me, Jericho."

Shuddering, he gave her what she wanted, coming hot and fast inside her. His eyes closed, and he groaned, the sound rough and helpless. "I love you. I've loved you since that very first night. I love you so fucking much it's enough to kill me again."

Shock punched her in the belly, knocked the breath out of her lungs. Then reaction kicked in. The agony was like ripping open a festering wound that had never healed. Bitter rage screamed through her, blackened her vision and she heaved underneath him. "Untie me, Jericho! Untie me *right now.*"

His reaction was immediate. He lunged for the scarves that bound her, letting her loose. She jackknifed on the bed, scrambling to get away from him. He caught her wrist to steady her when she tripped over the tangled bedspread. "*Don't touch me,*" she shrieked, ripping her arm from his grip. "Don't you touch me ever again."

"Okay. Okay, let's just be calm for a second." He lifted his hands in a placating gesture, wariness and hurt flashing in his gaze. "I'm confused by what's happening here. I told you I loved you and—"

"*Liar.*" The word exploded from her throat. "You *never* loved me. Never. Don't even try to feed me that line of bullshit. Those words never crossed your lips, not once. Don't try to rewrite the past, Jericho. I was there."

"Never loved you?" His laugh was an ugly, painful sound. "Hell, woman, I never *stopped* loving you. I couldn't. And God help me, I tried."

"Right," she sneered. Tears stung her eyes, but she blinked them back. She wouldn't cry in front of him, and he sure as hell didn't deserve her tears. He wanted to have this out? Drag the past into the present? Fine. Jericho always got what he wanted anyway, so she might as well give it to him. With both barrels. "That's why I found you in a brothel, draped across a prostitute's bed. If I remember it right—*and I do*—you left me with Enrique and never bothered looking back. Yeah, you *loved* me. You loved me so much, you couldn't even go a whole night without a woman to warm up the bed. You *never stopped loving me*, but I sure was easy to replace, wasn't I?"

Fury flushed his face, and he loomed over her, every muscle in his body taut with rage. "That wasn't what happened. I never even looked at another woman, let alone touched one while we were together. I took you back to your brother like you wanted, and I was so fucking miserable about it, I got drunk enough that I couldn't see straight. Hell, I don't even know how I got up the stairs to the room you found me in. I passed out, and I didn't wake up until you came to get me. *Nothing else happened.*"

Her laugh was every bit as horrible as his had been. God, she hated herself for still loving him. Her voice was little more than a scathing hiss, bile burning the back of her throat. "Nothing happened in a prostitute's bed? Sure. Of course. Right. That's an easy claim to make now, but I know what I saw."

"You know what you think you saw. You know what you wanted to see." He caught her arms, and she tried to jerk back, but he tightened his grip, giving her a little shake. "And that was always our problem, wasn't it? Hell, it's *still* our problem. You don't trust me. Sure, you'll give me your body, you'll come for me so often I don't know how either of us is walking straight, but you'll never *believe in me*. Believe in *us*. You may have *said* you loved me back then, but you've spent every second we were ever together, then and now, just waiting for the other shoe to drop, waiting for me to hurt you, waiting for me to leave you, waiting for us to fail. The only person you actually trusted was your yellow-bellied *coward* of a brother."

"You leave Enrique out of this!" She tried to wrench herself from his grasp again, but couldn't. He was too strong, and she had to settle for glaring at him. "The man's been dead for a hundred years or more, and you still have to attack him. The only thing I ever asked you for was to not hurt him, but you denied me, said you'd kill him without a second thought. So, tell me, Jericho, exactly what did you ever do to make me *trust* you? We were enemies, and you made it very clear I was a sexual convenience. I'm sure you enjoyed ruining my reputation to spite my brother. It was always about you and him, wasn't it? It was never about you and me. There was no *us* to believe in. I was just a pawn in the game you two were playing."

His silver eyes blazed to liquid mercury, and he shook her again, harder this time, his breath bellowing from his lungs. "You make me *insane.* You did then, and you do now. I couldn't keep my mind on anything but you, let alone figuring out how to dick with your brother's mind. I should have known his attack was coming, but I let myself get distracted by you."

"So now you're blaming me for your death?" Despite herself, tears sprang into her eyes. She blinked them back and finally managed to squirm out of his grasp. Her legs felt like limp noodles, so she stumbled to the end of the bed, grabbing the footboard for support. She looked up at him, and let herself ask the questions that had nagged at her for over a century. "*Why*, Jericho? Why didn't you leave when I told you to? I sacrificed so much to go to you, to save you. I betrayed my country, I betrayed my only family. I *died* to give you the chance to live. Why didn't you run? Was it really so important to kill Enrique? Was it worth your life?"

She expected him to spout some bullshit about honor and duty and standing his ground and not being a coward, but instead he met her gaze head on. "I did run. We were outnumbered, and I knew it. I told my men to retreat, put my lieutenant in charge, and then I chased after you. They were overtaken anyway, but...I was coming for *you*, not to kill your brother."

"Wh-what?" Of all the things he could have said, that stunned her the most. Jericho would never admit to abandoning his men to an inferior officer. Unless it was true. She shook her head, tried to pin down her reeling thoughts.

"But to answer your earlier question—no, I don't blame you for my death. I blame your brother, since he's the one who killed me."

All the blood drained from her face and she clenched her fingers into the iron footboard. "No. No, he couldn't have."

"He sure as hell could have. He *did*."

"It—it had to have been an accident." She swayed where she stood, her stomach twisting into knots. "He knew how I felt about you. He would never have done such a thing."

Jericho snorted. "You have no idea how much I would have given for even an ounce of that trust, but the truth is what it is, darlin'. Enrique put a bullet in me. He knew it was me, and whether he knew you loved me or not, it was no accident."

He had to be wrong. It had to be a mistake. Enrique had been devoted to her, and she'd worshipped him. She couldn't have been so wrong about him. They couldn't both have betrayed her. "Stop. P-please, stop."

His pewter eyes flashed. "I did what you asked. I didn't go after your brother. And when he found me holding your dead body in my arms, he shot me like I was a rabid animal because I refused to give you to him."

"*Noooo.*" The word was a low, keening plea. Not that. Please, God. Anything but that. Her fingers fisted in her hair, trying to block out the truth. She'd begged him, pleaded with him to leave her brother alone. Her last remaining family member, her blood. And it had cost him his life. She'd murdered the only man she'd ever loved as surely as if she'd pulled the trigger herself. Shame curled her spine, and she buried her face in her hands. "It's my fault. It's my fault. Oh, *God*. I failed you and it's all my fault. We died because of *me*."

"No." He wrapped his arms around her from behind, his lips nuzzling the nape of her neck. "No, Tori, it's *my* fault. *I* failed *you*. I should never have let you walk out of that saloon in the first place, but I was too hurt that you didn't trust me not to cheat on you, that you dared to have any doubts, that you needed an explanation. I was too stubborn to see that if I'd just reached out to you then, given you what you needed, I might have had everything I ever wanted. But I couldn't swallow my pride enough to tell you that you were everything, and I let you leave thinking you were nothing." He crushed her to him, squeezing her so tight he compressed her ribs. Almost as if he never intended to let her go again, and a sob ripped from her throat at the thought. "It would have cost me so little, just a few words, but I was too fucking stupid to see it. So, we both died. I watched the life drain out of you, and I still never told you I loved you. I've been waiting a long, long time to say those words."

"Jericho." His name was a breathy sob on her lips. She didn't know what else to say, what else to do. He was right— she'd never really trusted him, not all the way, not with everything. She'd trusted her brother instead, and she'd been wrong. "If I had only—"

"No." His soft lips brushed her shoulder. "No more of that. No more worrying about failure. No more blame. We both did things we regret. A lot of things. But we can't change the past. We can just move forward from here—and I want to move forward with you. I want a future." He swallowed audibly, and there was a hesitancy in his voice that she'd never heard before. "If—if you want me too."

"I...I..." Her mind spun in circles, far too much information jockeying for supremacy in her mind. Jericho had come after her that night. He'd *cared.* Tears slid down her face as deep sobs wrenched out of her. He rocked her in his arms, crooning soft comfort to her, just...holding her. Somewhere in that dark and ugly storm of guilt and realization, some fragile fragment of joy began to surface. Her soul mate hadn't betrayed her; he'd *loved* her. He still loved her, and he was here, now, with her.

They had a second chance, if only she dared to reach out and take it, if only she was willing to trust it.

Trust. It had always come down to trust, just like he'd said. Trust, and her fear of failure. Pain cinched around her heart at all the time they'd lost, at the *life* they'd lost. In their own ways, they'd both been unable to truly believe in their love enough to reach out, to make that final step, and it had cost them. But they didn't have to repeat those mistakes. They'd both learned, both grown in the time they'd been separated.

"I love you, Vitoria." He turned her to face him, his silver gaze open and more vulnerable than she'd ever imagined possible. He didn't hold back, everything he felt was there for her to see. His big hand smoothed her hair back. "My Tori. I love you. I always have. I always will. There was never anyone else. I would never betray you. *I love you.* If you don't believe anything else I ever say, believe that."

"I believe you," she whispered, tears still slipping down her cheeks. "I love you too."

His beautiful eyes closed, and the skin drew taut across his sharp cheekbones. "Say it again."

"I believe in you, Jericho." She reached up to curve her palms around his face, waiting for him to look at her again. "I believe in us. I love you. I never want to spend another day apart from you."

"I love you." He buried his nose against her temple, his lips brushing her ear. "God, how I love you."

She swallowed and let herself hold and be held by him, letting herself trust that their love could last, that they wouldn't fail this time. Just...letting herself absorb the miracle of him. She'd waited so long, needed him so much.

Leaning against his chest, she hugged him tight as sudden fear speared her. "Wait. We're not human anymore. Do you think we'll be *allowed* to stay together?"

"Oh, yeah." He smiled against her skin. "The Big Man wants soul mates to be with each other—look at what we do for a living. We're working together from now on."

"How can you be sure?" If Heaven compelled them to go to different jobs, that was that. Guardian angels didn't get a say in these things. Her heart sank, tears filling her eyes. To have found him again, only to be forced to separate, would be more than she could bear.

He chuckled, the sound rich and warm, and it made her toes curl. "Because I had two assignments, darlin'. Celia...and you."

Make Me Believe

Dedication

This one is for all the people who've emailed me asking for Celia and Mason's book. Thanks for enjoying the first two books in the series enough to want a third.

Chapter One

Cedarville, Oregon

How did she get herself into these messes? Oh, right. She had friends with the utter gall to be *happy.*

Celia Occam rolled her eyes and tried to ignore the fact that she was up to her eyeballs in decorations for her best friend's surprise wedding reception. Aubrey had eloped with her new husband Price a few weeks before, without any of the frills of a real wedding, so a surprise party to celebrate the occasion was in order. Actually, the owner of the local bed and breakfast inn had insisted on throwing the shindig and had roped Celia into helping put it together. Silver balloons and navy blue streamers hung from every surface of the B&B.

"Give me a hand with this, won't you, dear?" Mrs. Chambers called. The elderly woman—and certified small town busybody—wobbled on top of a stepladder, the white knot coiled on top of her head wobbling even more precariously.

Celia's heart tripped when she saw the old lady go up on her tiptoes to string more streamers from a doorway. "Get *down*, Mrs. Chambers."

"Oh, I can do it. Just hold—"

"No, ma'am." She leaped up from where she knelt attaching a table skirt, jogging over to brace the other woman's legs. "Please, stop. I can take care of it for you. Really. Come away from there."

"If you insist." Climbing down with more grace than Celia would have imagined, Mrs. Chambers brushed off her dress. Then she wagged her finger. "I've told you to call me Tori."

"Right. Tori." Celia sighed in relief at having the older woman on solid ground, grabbed the dangling end of the streamer and hopped up on the ladder while Tori watched. "I might slip and call you Mrs. C sometimes, Mrs. C."

"So I see." Tori laughed, but then her tone turned coy and teasing. "Mason Delacroix is coming to the party tonight."

Celia's heart thumped at the mention of his name. She stomped down on the reaction, ignoring it as she had for the year she'd known him. Forcing her voice into nonchalance, she busied herself with hanging more paper doodads. "Well, he's the groom's brother, so I assumed you invited him."

"He's such a nice young man. Handsome too." Tori handed her a piece of tape for the next streamer. "I think he likes you."

"I think he'd just like to get in my pants," Celia muttered.

"What was that, dear?"

"Nothing." She glanced down and smiled as innocently as she could, which wasn't very, but she gave it a shot.

Tori's white bun teetered when she tilted her head and narrowed her eyes. Lately, she'd been hell-bent in her mission to fix Celia and Mason up, and she fired a new salvo. "He'd be good for you, and he *does* like you. You should take him up on it the next time he asks you out. He's not going to your hair salon just for his looks."

Of course, everyone knew Mason made appointments at Occam's Razor to have her shave his head on a regular basis. Each time he'd come in, he'd asked her out. But he hadn't come in the last few weeks, and his hair had grown into a dark stubble. It did nothing to detract from his good looks. Tori was right about that... Mason was undeniably handsome.

When Celia didn't respond, Tori heaved a dramatically disappointed sigh. "I'll just go see if Jerry needs help in the kitchen."

"You do that." Celia shook her head as the town gossip

bustled away, reluctant affection winding through her. Mrs. Chambers got her hair washed and styled at Celia's salon at least three times a week, just for an excuse to eavesdrop on any juicy conversations that might be going on. The woman knew everything about everyone—her abilities in that arena never failed to impress Celia. Spending a good portion of her childhood in Cedarville meant everyone knew everything about Celia's sordid past already, so she didn't have to worry about what Tori might hear about her. Ah, small town life.

While she twisted and taped up the crinkled paper decorations, she could hear the sound of Tori talking to Jerry. The flamingly gay man was Celia's newest stylist, and he'd struck up a tight friendship with the gossipy biddy that she couldn't begin to understand. But as long as they were happy, Celia wasn't about to question it. She'd figured out long ago that it was best to enjoy the moment she was in, and worry as little as possible about things she couldn't change. If people were happy, it was all good.

"There," she said, affixing the last bunch of balloons to the corner of the doorframe. Clamoring off the stepladder, she executed a slow spin to take in the whole room. She propped her hands on her hips and grinned.

"It looks great," a deep voice rumbled from directly behind her.

A high-pitched squeak erupted from her throat, and she whipped around. "Damn it, Mason! Don't sneak up on people like that. Make a noise or something."

"I did make a noise. I said it looked great. Good to see you again, Celia." One dark eyebrow rose, but not an ounce of chagrin crossed his face. Instead, he just grinned at her, a slow, wicked smile that would make any woman's toes curl.

Any woman except her, damn it. She was immune, and that was final. Her body could just get with the program and stop melting down every time he came near her. She crossed her arms over her breasts to cover her beading nipples, which just drew his gaze down to her cleavage. A wave of heat sluiced through her, and she dropped her arms. "What are you doing here?"

If she sounded breathless and her heart beat too fast, she blamed on it the fact that he'd startled her. It was a lie and she knew it. The man was hot enough to be hazardous to her mental well being. Just having him this close made her pulse flutter. The truth was, the man was sex on a stick. At well over six foot tall, he was a solid wall of muscle. Then again, firefighters had to be in good shape. His sub-bass voice and emerald eyes just completed one scrumptious package. She cleared her throat, tearing her gaze away from every luscious inch of him. The last thing she wanted was to encourage him to come on to her. Again. He'd slacked off lately, and she shouldn't mess with that progress.

One of his broad shoulders dipped in a shrug, his smile never faltering. "Jerry asked me to come over early to help out. Price is my brother, after all."

Mrs. Chambers had done the same thing with her. Aubrey was Celia's best friend, after all. It was all she could do not to roll her eyes. From the moment she'd hired him, Jerry had jumped on Tori's bandwagon to try to hook Celia up with Mason. Why they were so interested in playing cupid, she had no clue. Her love life—or lack thereof—was no one's business but her own. Mason seemed amused by the extra help in his pursuit of her, which had been beyond persistent until recently.

She was firing Jerry's ass the moment she saw him again.

"Well, I'm sure they could use a hand bringing up bottles of champagne from the cellar. Jerry's not one for heavy lifting." Her *über*-effeminate employee never hefted anything weightier than a pair of trimming shears. She tossed her head and looked anywhere except at Mason. "People should start arriving in about half an hour."

He stepped closer, and a shiver of awareness went down her spine. His breath brushed against her skin when he spoke. "You look beautiful tonight."

Closing her eyes for a moment, she tried to suppress the longing that expanded inside her. This happened whenever he was near. Her hormones reminded her how long it had been since she'd had a man moving over her, in her. She could only be thankful that he didn't touch her, that he'd never reached for her. It had taken everything inside Celia not to give in all these months. Her sanity might not survive if he pushed any harder, but her body's needs had nothing to do with reason or sanity. She pulled in a slow breath, inhaling the potent masculine scent of him. She had to get away from him before she jumped him. Scuttling back, she turned to face him. "Thank you. It's a new dress."

"Only you could pull off combat boots with a dress and make it look good." He chuckled, the sound rich and warm. It made her want to rip his clothes off, throw him to the ground, and have her way with him.

She stuck her foot out, trying desperately *not* to think about things that might encourage her wayward hormones. "Knee high, shiny blue patent leather combat boots, thank you very much. The blue makes all the difference."

"I'll take your word for it. It works for you." His eyes narrowed as he looked her over. "You changed your hair."

Her hand rose to touch her hair self-consciously, but she stopped herself and lifted her chin. "Yep, I did. A stylist has to update so her clients see her versatility."

"It's cute. I like the red."

Her insides warmed at the compliment, and she stomped down those soft emotions. "Thanks. You seem to be changing your style too."

Whether she meant growing his hair or halting his quest to

get her to sleep with him, she wasn't sure. As much as she hated to admit it, even to herself, she'd missed his visits to her salon. When he wasn't doggedly set on breaking down her defenses, he was an entertaining person to have around. She sighed. That seemed to be the biggest problem for her. When it came to Mason, she never knew if she was coming or going. Hell, she didn't know if *he* was coming or going. What did he want from her? What did she want from him?

He scrubbed a hand over his stubbled head. "Yeah, well... Sometimes change is a good thing. Makes people see your versatility."

And that was a direct hit. A chuckle bubbled out of her. "Right."

Charming, funny, even occasionally sweet. Also a sarcastic, stubborn pain in the backside.

At first, she'd thought he'd pursued her seriously. She'd even once told Aubrey he was the marrying kind—and Celia had tried and failed at that *twice* now. But she'd heard him make disparaging remarks about matrimony. That, combined with his three short-lived engagements, told her he wasn't planning to commit to anyone anytime soon. Which was just as well, since she wasn't looking for that.

Then again, she wasn't looking for anything. Not even a date, which was just one of the many reasons she'd continued to turn him down this past year. The three broken engagements under his belt didn't speak well for how he handled relationships. She wasn't one to judge, considering her failed marriages, but as far as she could tell his persistence was about a boy being denied the toy he wanted to play with.

She had to wonder if his fiancées had resisted him, too, and he'd grown bored when he got what he wanted. The thought made her stomach twist. It did nothing to make her think she should go out with him.

She'd stopped dating after her last divorce and had no interest in a real relationship. Not that she slept around, but she had a few guys in town who were available when she had an itch to scratch. It kept things simpler that way. They weren't interested in more and neither was she. It was safer than trying to pretend this was going somewhere it wasn't. Relationships tended to be a one-way freight train toward marriage, so why bother faking it?

No way in hell was she getting married again. Ever.

"Are you sure there's nothing in here I can help you with?" His voice startled her out of her musings. "Everything already looks great."

His gaze moved around the room, taking in the decorations, the empty buffet tables, and the fancy Victorian décor of the B&B. Then he looked her over just as thoroughly, and heat touched her everywhere his gaze went.

"Um..." She swallowed, scrambling to think of something non-pornographic that he could help her with. Chemistry was such a bitch. She gestured to the tables. "I'm guessing Tori wants those loaded up."

"Tori?"

"Mrs. Chambers. She's decided I can call her by her first name."

"Huh." He folded his arms, and his shirt molded to his heavy chest. "I didn't even know she had a first name. I mean, obviously she *has* one, but I've never heard anybody use it."

"Yeah, the first person I ever heard use it was Jerry." She turned and headed toward the kitchen. The longer she stood staring at his flexing arms and feeling the magnetic pull he had on her, the more likely she was to do something stupid. Like offer to serve herself up as his personal naked buffet.

"Those two are quite the odd couple now, aren't they?" Affection echoed in his voice, and Celia glanced back to see a grin crinkling the corners of his eyes.

Jesus, the man needed to be licensed, his smile was that lethal. She forced herself to face forward again before she ran into something. But the quiet fondness in his expression also said he cared about the older lady, and that was...nice.

She shook her head at that kind of thinking. She had to be brutally honest about why she didn't want to go out with him, and it had little to do with her no-dating, no-relationship policy. The real problem had never been Mason, had it? No, the problem had always been that whenever Mason came near her, she started to dream of things that didn't exist. He was rock-solid, the kind of guy everyone could count on. The whole town knew he was the heir apparent for when the fire chief retired in a few years. He was big, strong, good-looking, sexy as hell and a *nice* guy. He was perfect, a modern day Prince Charming. The type of man every woman wanted in her life and in her bed. Forever.

And forever wasn't on Celia's agenda. There was no such thing, at least not in her experience. So, she wasn't going to pretend there was, and she didn't want anything to do with a man who made her fantasize about it. That was just emotional suicide in the making, and she refused to go there. It wasn't his fault, and she wished he'd taken no for an answer the first time he'd asked her out.

In the end, it didn't matter if he was the marrying kind or if he just wanted to shag her brains out for a night. What mattered was that he made her *want* him to be the marrying kind, and that way lay disaster. She had the divorce papers to prove it. Two sets of them. She couldn't risk letting him in, even for a night.

Most of the time, she'd just bang him and hope that got him out of her system, but the chemistry with Mason was way too explosive for that. Without even trying, he was dangerous. Nope. No way. No how. She wasn't going there.

If there was one thing any idiot knew, it was that people who played with fire got burned.

"Price is the best brother anyone could ask for, and one of the best men I know. No one is more worthy of happiness than he is, and I couldn't be happier for him." For a moment, Mason almost looked like he was going to get choked up, but his hand tightened on his champagne flute and he flashed a brilliant smile. "And since Aubrey is as intelligent as she is gorgeous, she knows that even the best men appreciate what they have to work for, so she gave him a run for his money." Anyone who had witnessed the couple's tumultuous courtship knew that was the understatement of the century. Laughter rolled through the small gathering at the party, a few people letting out wolf whistles. "But in the end, I think they both got what they deserved. Each other. So, if you'll all raise your glasses with me. To Price and Aubrey."

"To Price and Aubrey," the crowd echoed.

Even though marriage wasn't Celia cup of tea, she couldn't help the way her throat closed at the expression of open adoration on her best friend's face. And Price looked no less besotted.

Jesus, she was going soft. She leaned her hip up against a nearby table, coughed and took a deep swig of the bubbly. The institution of marriage hadn't done well by her, but for her friend's sake, she hoped this one lasted. Then again, until Price, Aubrey had been as cynical about matrimony as Celia. A cheating ex tended to turn a girl bitter.

"Excuse me." Mason appeared beside her and offered that same over-bright smile, but it couldn't hide the shadows in his eyes. The grin crumbled after a moment, and he scooped up the champagne bottle from the table beside her to refill his flute. A muscle ticked in his jaw. "Mrs. Chambers and Jerry know how to throw a great party."

Her eyebrows drew together as she watched his closed expression. An unexpected dart of concern went through her. Mason was usually the more easygoing and cheerful of the Delacroix brothers, so his seriousness at such a joyous occasion was more that a little strange. "You okay?"

"Great. I'm...great."

"Great. Can I get another word?"

He huffed out a laugh and downed half his booze. "I'll be fine. I'm happy for my brother, but these kinds of events aren't really my thing."

"I hear you." She tapped his glass with hers, empathy twisting inside her. Yeah, she could see how three broken engagements would make this sort of party salt on the wound for him. She could relate—and sympathy for Mason was the last thing she'd expected tonight, which just made the *Twilight Zone* experience of being at a wedding reception that much freakier. "I usually avoid them like the plague. But for Aubrey..."

"Yeah." He sighed. "For Price."

He shifted where he stood, his arm brushing hers. It was like touching a live wire. Tingles skipped from her shoulder down to her fingers and up again, spreading throughout her body. Fire flowed in the wake of the tingles. It was ridiculous, the way this man got to her. Too bad he was too dangerous to play with. Clearing her throat, she looked away and made herself focus on something else.

"Everyone besides us is loving this though." She looked around at the bright lights, the laughing people, the happy couple. Music played and couples danced. It was loud and boisterous and exactly what a party like this should be. Good for Aubrey and Price, bad for those who had nothing but ugly memories associated with marriage.

"Of course, they are. I know how to entertain." Mrs. Chambers's tart voice preceded her as she bustled up to the table to survey the spread of tasty food. She peered inside the champagne bottle. "Though I become far less entertaining when there's nothing to help the guests loosen up."

"You mean loosen up their tongues so they start telling you all their dirty little secrets, don't you, Tori?" Celia winked at the older woman, who had the good grace to blush.

She swatted Celia's arm. "For that, young lady, you can go down to the basement and fetch more champagne."

"Yes, ma'am." Celia saluted her with her glass before she set it on the table. A few minutes away from the lovefest would be a bit of a relief.

Tori cast a severe glance at Mason. "And you'll be a gentleman and help her."

His dark brows rose, his eyes twinkling with sudden humor. He bowed gallantly. "Yes, *ma'am.*"

She snagged his champagne flute and flapped her free hand at him. "Go on, now. Don't tease an innocent, harmless old lady."

He laughed in her face, grabbed the hand she waved at him, and kissed the back of it. "I wouldn't dream of it, ma'am."

Sweeping an arm out in front of him, he motioned Celia forward. She rolled her eyes at their antics and spun toward the kitchen. "We'll be back in a few minutes. Let Aubrey know if she wonders where I've disappeared to, would you?"

"I will."

Mason fell into step behind her, close enough that she could feel his body heat against her back. They entered the kitchen, and he reached around her to open the cellar door. "You realize she's trying to get us alone together."

"Yeah, Mrs. C isn't exactly subtle." She glanced over her shoulder at him, the little grin on his lips making her heart trip. Desire twisted within her. She *wanted* those lips on hers, had wanted it for months. She shook herself, turned away and flipped on the switch to flood the basement with light. Hustling down the stairs, she looked around for the case of champagne. What looked like a beat up and discarded set of living room furniture was pushed up against one wall, a few tarnished silver dishes on the coffee table. Boxes and crates were piled haphazardly all over the place, one of them marked with the brand of bubbly Mrs. Chambers was serving. "I've resisted you for a year, Delacroix. I don't think an old lady's matchmaking is going to change that."

His heavy tread echoed as he followed her down the steps. "I don't encourage her. I only encouraged you."

"You don't discourage her, either." She pointed him toward the wooden crate of champagne.

He snorted as he waved her aside and lifted the case by himself, the muscles in his arms bulging. "As if I could. She has her nose in everyone's business, but she's not hurting anyone. Some people are vicious with gossip—she just likes to know everything. Besides, it's not like she can force you to do anything with me, right?"

"Right." She sighed. "She's pretty harmless, I know. It's just a little annoying at times. I'm ready for her to stick her nose in someone else's love life now. Is that too much to ask?"

The door above them slammed shut, a distinct click sounding as a lock engaged.

Mason's jaw sagged open for a moment, and he set the champagne back down with a loud *thunk*. "Oh, no fucking way. She wouldn't."

"Shit!" Celia bolted up the stairs, twisting the doorknob, though she knew it was useless. She pounded her fist on the door, disbelief and desperation screaming through her. This couldn't be happening. It couldn't. "Come *on*, Mrs. Chambers. This isn't funny."

"There's no way out of there except through this door, so don't bother trying to find one. You're trapped until we say otherwise." Jerry's distinctive lisp came through the thick wood. "Take the opportunity to get to know each other. It'll be fun!"

Chapter Two

"You are *fired*, Jerry." She kicked the door with her combat boot for good measure, though she knew none of the guests would hear over the music, and her evil cupids wouldn't care. She stomped down a few of the stairs before turning to shout even louder, just for the pleasure of venting her spleen. "The moment I get out of here, you're getting booted from my salon, Jerry! Believe it. And *Tori* can get her hair done somewhere else!"

There was no response, of course, and all she could do was stare at the door in impotent rage, willing it to open and knowing it wouldn't. She was stuck here. Trapped. She closed her eyes. "I don't have my cell phone with me. It's in my purse, which Jerry put away in a spare room when I got here."

"My cell's in my coat pocket, and Mrs. Chambers took that. All I have is my work pager."

Frustration tangled with...fear in her chest. The last thing she wanted was to be alone with Mason. She'd done everything in her power in the last year to make sure that *never* happened. Her fingers balled into fists at her sides. Damn it. Damn *them*. And their meddling.

She turned and found him right behind her. Scrabbling backward to keep from touching him, the backs of her calves hit the next stair up, and she tripped and slammed into the railing sideways. Her arms flailed, her heart stopping in her chest, a short scream wrenching from her throat, and she would have gone over the rail if he hadn't grabbed her. She hung there for a moment, staring at the long drop down to the hard cement floor. All the blood rushed out of her face so fast, it tingled with cold shock.

He hauled her up against his chest, lifted her and spun to press her against the wall. Which meant she ended up exactly where she hadn't wanted to be. In his arms. "Are you all right?"

No, she wasn't. It felt as if all the oxygen had been sucked out of the room. She couldn't even breathe, her heart slammed so hard against her sternum. The chill fled her limbs in a split-second, the fire that flooded her as shocking as her near tragedy.

Clenching her fingers in the front of his shirt, she shuddered, too many sensations bombarding her at once. Terror still made her shake, but God, she was plastered against him from breast to thigh and her nerve endings rioted. Every inch of her reacted to him. Her skin flushed, her nipples tightened to thrust against her bra and the folds of her sex went hot and slick.

Somehow, she had known it would be this intense. If standing next to him or cutting his hair could rev her up, being sandwiched between the hard wall and his hard body was enough to cause a nuclear meltdown.

"I'm fine, thanks. You can let me go now." It took everything ounce of willpower she had to gasp those two short sentences.

His gaze locked on her lips as she spoke. "I can't."

"What do you mean, you *can't?*" The words came out in a rush, almost tripping over each other.

He drew in a deep breath, which rubbed her breasts against his chest. God, she could feel every ripple of muscle in his body. He was even better built than she'd imagined. "I can't let you go when you're looking at me like that. I've been dying to taste you for months, and I have to know what it's like. I'm sorry."

Any response she might have made was smothered by his mouth. She tensed, waiting to be all but consumed, devoured, taken. It didn't happen.

His kiss was a gentle savoring. The way his body pressed her into the wall, hard enough to compress her ribs, became an erotic contrast to the sweetness of his lips on hers. His tongue teased her lower lip, easing into her mouth. The flavor of him exploded over her taste buds, headier than the champagne they'd drunk. Any resistance fled under the onslaught of yearning. She moaned, twining her tongue with his, fighting with him for control of the kiss.

Straining against him, she writhed to get even closer. He groaned, releasing her mouth to string kisses down her jaw and throat. She let her head fall back against the wall, arching mindlessly when his teeth scored the sensitive tendon that connected neck to shoulder.

"Mason, please." She cupped the back of his head, holding him to her. His short hair prickled her palms, and she dug her nails into his scalp, desperate for more. *"More."*

Unfastening the side zipper on her dress, he slipped his hand inside to stroke her ribs. She shivered, her nipples pinching tight. She wanted his mouth on them, but she couldn't make her mind and her tongue work together to form the demand.

Slipping down to bracket her hips with his palms, he gathered her dress one handful at a time. His fingertips brushed her skin, tracing the edge of her panties. Her flesh burned everywhere their bodies met, her pussy weeping juices. It was too much, and not enough, all at the same time. The more he touched her, the more she craved it. Him.

"I want you, Celia. Now." His arms went around her again, pulling her off her feet. She wrapped her legs around his waist, mating her sex with his through their clothing. His palms curved under her ass, squeezing the soft globes and making her squirm against him. He groaned and staggered down the rest of the stairs. Each step rubbed his cock over her pussy, and her core contracted on an emptiness that needed to be filled.

The couch cushions were soft under her back as he laid her there. From the corner of her eye, she noticed the champagne bottle protruding out of one of the silver bowls. It was chilling on ice, and two glasses sat beside it. Turning her head, she saw strawberries in another dish and some of the *hors d'oeuvres* from the party piled in another. The final bowl was filled with a colorful array of condoms.

A note card propped against the strawberry container read:

Kick back and have all the fun you can manage. You might as well since we aren't springing you until morning. Love, Your Guardian Angels.

The handwriting was in Jerry's distinctive scrawl. Celia snorted and rolled her eyes. "Guardian angels, my ass. Prison guards is more like it."

Mason barely glanced at the offerings. "I have better things to worry about than an old lady and a gay hairdresser right now."

He leaned away from her, his faced flushed with lust, his skin drawn taut across his sharp cheekbones. His jaw clenched, his gaze intent as he stripped her bare. Tugging her dress away from her shoulders, he slipped it down her body.

"Lift your hips," he whispered.

She did, arching off the sofa. He drew her dress and sheer black panties down her thighs, over her boots and off her legs. He tossed them behind him and paused as he took in her equally sheer mesh bra and black lacy thigh high stockings. He grinned and shook his head. Then he worked on her bra, unhooking the clasp at the front and helping her pull it off her arms.

"The boots and stockings can stay. They're sexy." He bent forward and kissed her calf just above the top of one boot.

It was a moment that could have come straight out of every fantasy she'd ever had about him. She swallowed. "Maybe this isn't such a good—"

"Nuh-uh. No backing out now." Bending farther, he buried his face in the thatch of hair at the apex of her thighs. His tongue dipped in, flicking over her clit.

Shock sizzled through her system, and he pressed her thighs flat to the cushions, taking as much access as he could get. His mouth settled on her clit and sucked hard, and she cried out. Fire danced over her skin, and still it wasn't enough to satisfy her. Her hands curved around her breasts, fingers circling her nipples. It added another layer to the overwhelming sensations, and she wanted more.

He pulled back, his eyes wild, her wetness glistening on his lips. "I have to have you now."

The man stripped in a few seconds, dropping his pager to the table before his clothes hit the floor. She would have teased him about his eagerness, but she was more than ready for him to be naked. And inside her. His bare body was as tightly muscled as she'd imagined, a thin sprinkling of hair bisecting his chest and trailing down to the hard curve of his cock. He was big. It was the only thought she had before he tore open one of the condoms, slid it on with rough efficiency and was on top of her, his thighs wedging hers open wider. The smooth head of his dick probed at her pussy, and she shoved upward. She couldn't wait, she needed him moving within her. He filled her, stretched her to the limits and then some.

A low cry burst from her throat, her hands clutching at his shoulders. Her nails dug into his flesh as she struggled to accommodate his girth. When he was seated to the hilt inside her, he groaned, his arms shaking as they braced on either side of her. "Are you okay?"

She nodded, renewed urgency beginning to wind inside her, the sharpness of it a blade that shredded her control. Her grip tightened on his shoulders, her hips undulating in a mindless drive to communicate her need. "Don't stop."

His laugh was harsh. "Sweetheart, I'm not sure I could."

Rocking his pelvis against her, he drove her to madness. She wrapped her legs around his lean hips. Her body bowed, trying to take him deeper, make him move faster, *anything* that would grant her the surcease only he could give her. Squeezing her inner muscles around his cock, she smiled when he shuddered and groaned. And thrust hard, giving her what she craved.

He did it again. And again, picking up speed and force with each entry. Pleasure exploded through her when he slammed into her body, their flesh slapping, the carnal sound of sex echoing in the basement. He dipped down to capture her lips, his tongue thrusting into her mouth with the same rhythm his body set for hers. She moaned and slid her palms over his flexing his arms and shoulders, loving the play of his rougher skin against hers, loving the way they moved together. The way the hair on his chest rasped across her nipples, his musky masculine scent filled her nostrils, his hips rubbed hard against her clit, his mouth worshipped hers—it drove her closer and closer to climax.

God, it was incredible, just as she'd always feared it would be.

Each time he pushed his long dick into her pussy, her channel spasmed. She could feel her orgasm building. Sweat slipped down her skin, her lungs burning as she sucked in oxygen. Pleasure flowed through her in waves, gaining force until it was a tsunami that threatened to drag her under. She clung to him, to sanity. It was too much to handle, terrifying

147

and beautiful all at once. Her nails dug into his back and he hissed, pounding his cock into her sex, pushing them both over the edge.

When he ground down into her clit, she exploded into climax. A scream ripped from her throat, lost under the commanding pressure of his mouth on hers. There was no escaping the shattering ecstasy of it. Her pussy flexed around his cock, again and again. Tingles broke down her skin, her body consumed by sensations that were too hot to contain.

He shoved deep inside her, deeper than he'd been before, and she screamed and came again. He threw his head back and froze above her, shuddering as orgasm took him as well. *"Celia!"*

A moan was the only response she could make. He collapsed on top of her, his heavy weight crushing her into the couch cushions. It felt good. She ran her fingertips up and down his back as the dampness evaporated from their skin, as their breathing and heart rates slowed to normal. Time drifted, everything hazy with repletion. He stroked her bare hip, his face nuzzling into the crook of her neck. His warm breath against her skin made her sigh.

He groaned and slid his softening cock out of her. A shiver she couldn't stop coursed through her at the glide of flesh. He swallowed as he sat beside her hip on the couch. His hand curved around her thigh, his gaze looking a little blurry and shell shocked. "Are you okay?"

"I think so. You?"

"Yeah." He blinked and a satiated grin curved his lips. "Definitely."

"Well, okay then."

Rubbing his thumb across the top of her leg, he glanced around and sighed when he spotted the bathroom door. He bent forward and brushed a kiss just above her navel. "I'm going to clean up. I'll be right back."

"Take your time. I'm not going anywhere." She sat up and watched him walk toward the small half-bath, his buttocks flexing with every step. Damn, he was a good-looking man.

Somewhere in the back of her mind, she knew she should be kicking her own ass for giving in to temptation, for not telling him no. He would have listened if she'd insisted, she knew he would have, but the bottom line was, she'd wanted this for a long time. She just hadn't wanted the emotional complications that might come along with it.

Well, too late for regrets.

She shook her head at herself and reached for one of the strawberries. If she were stuck here for the night, she'd enjoy the moment and worry about the morning when it arrived. It would get here sooner than she'd like, and then she'd deal with the consequences of tonight's choices. She didn't want to think about it now. At all.

The fruit's flavor burst inside her mouth, the sweet pulp and seeds melting on her tongue. She closed her eyes and sighed, savoring the simple act of chewing. It was a pure, sensual experience, like everything else since they'd been locked down here.

A choked sound made her eyes fly open. Mason stood in the bathroom doorway, his gaze locked on her mouth. His face was tight with lust, and his Adam's apple bobbed when he swallowed. "I've never gotten hard just watching someone eat a strawberry."

He wasn't lying. His erection curved to just below his navel, and her sex fisted looking at him. He strode toward her, his gaze glinting with a promise she now knew he could more than fulfill. She shuddered, heat swamped her and renewed moisture flooded her pussy. If he'd never been turned on watching someone eat, she'd never gotten hot watching a man move across the room.

But, Jesus. The man was a walking felony, and she could appreciate it more now that he wasn't on top of her. His shoulders were impossibly broad, his legs long and thick—his entire body was a tightly packed symphony of muscle. Heavy pecs were sprinkled with dark hair, and she wanted to lick those flat brown nipples. His abs formed hard ridges that her fingers itched to stroke.

She curled her fingers into balls to keep from touching him as something occurred to her. She nodded toward his pager. "Don't you have to go in to work at a god-awful time in the morning? What if they don't let us out in time?"

"I'm not really thinking about work right now." He huffed out a laugh, gesturing down at his aroused body. "But since you're interested, I have tomorrow off."

Her brows drew together. "But...tomorrow's Thursday."

His broad shoulder lifted in a shrug. "Firefighters' schedules are weird. We go twenty-four hours on, forty-eight hours off."

"So, you're there for twenty-four hours straight?"

Amusement glimmered in his gaze, but he answered her anyway. "Yep, we eat there, sleep there. Just waiting for an emergency call to come in."

"Huh. You're right. That is weird." Even weirder was that she was having a perfectly normal conversation with him. While stark naked. It was like an erotic dream mixed with an out of body experience.

He cleared his throat, shifting his weight. "Some women don't like the schedule."

The odd inflection in his voice had her tilting her head back to look him in the face. "You've dated women like that?"

"As it turns out, I was engaged to one." His tone was easy,

conveying that whatever had happened, he'd come to an acceptance of it.

"I take it that wasn't the fiancée who was also a firefighter." When his eyebrows arched, she hastened to add, "Tori told me. I didn't ask."

"Of course not." He smirked at her, reaching out to run a possessive hand down her bare shoulder to her breast. "You would never ask about me—you have no interest in me."

"Nope. None." She walked her fingers up his chest and tweaked his nipple. Hard.

"Hey!" He jerked, slapping a hand over hers, a laugh rippling out of him.

She flattened her palm, feeling the bump of his heartbeat. "But seriously... What happens if there's an emergency tonight and you get paged to come in?"

His tone turned matter-of-fact. "If it comes to it, I will rip that door off its hinges."

"You can't do that now?" Though the question was a bit like closing the barn door after the horse had escaped.

"Nope, I like being locked down here with you." He grinned. "Plus, Mrs. Chambers would make me come back to clean up the mess and fix her door. No thanks, I'll stick it out unless it becomes necessary to do otherwise."

She scowled up at him. "I don't like being held hostage."

Taking the remainder of the strawberry from her, he slid the fruit over her bottom lip, leaving a trail of sweet stickiness. Then he bent down to lick the juices away. "Let me take your mind off of it."

Chapter Three

Celia stepped out of her salon and closed the door behind her. She loved Occam's Razor. Focusing on growing her business had gotten her through some of the darkest days of her life, so she was more than a little proud of its success. She'd bought the entire building, kept the old charm of the original barbershop on the bottom floor and, after her second divorce, moved into the apartment on the top floor.

Passing by the spinning red, white, and blue barbershop pole, she jogged across the street to the park that made up the town square. Aubrey had called to ask her to come over for lunch, and her best friend's coffee shop was on the far side of the square. Celia smoothed her hair and her clothes as she walked along one of the many paths that wound through the park. A quick shower was all she'd managed before she'd had to open the shop for her first customer, but she assured herself that there was nothing in her appearance that indicated she'd spent the night having a shagfest with Mason.

Lucky for Jerry, he'd called in sick today. Maybe when he decided he felt better, she'd be less inclined to give him the boot.

She came around a copse of trees and spotted the sign for Aubrey's shop, Bean There, Done That. Looking both ways, Celia crossed the street, the aroma of coffee luring her in like a Lorelei. No one made coffee and baked goods like Aubrey. She'd been a pastry chef at a fancy restaurant in Portland before her first marriage crumbled and she'd moved to Cedarville. Portland's loss was Cedarville's gain.

And Celia had gotten a best friend out of the arrangement, so she couldn't complain.

Pushing open the door, she saw Aubrey and her assistant behind the counter, a short line queuing up to order. Aubrey waved her into the rear of the shop, so Celia walked through the swinging door that led to a large room where a huge prep table dominated the space. Ovens lined an entire wall, the scent of fresh pastries filling the air. Celia pulled up a stool at the table and plopped down.

"Hey, hon." Aubrey hustled in, carrying a silver baking pan which had plates and cups of coffee balanced on it. She set the food and drinks in front of Celia, then dropped the pan into a huge basin sink. "All right. Susan will come get me if the crowd gets too bad, but it looks like we have a lull, so I can take a break."

"Great." Two of the plates had a nice little green salad and a turkey and cheese croissant sandwich, and a third plate was piled with cookies. Celia picked up her sandwich and dug in. She moaned when it hit her taste buds. "Oh, man. This is so amazing. I swear you put crack on your food—you just can't stop eating it."

"It's the fresh croissant. Once you've had the real thing, you can't go back to the processed stuff."

"Crack sprinkled freshness. Nice."

"Hey, whatever keeps the business coming in." Aubrey laughed, sat and dug into her salad.

"You said it."

"So, how did last night go?" Aubrey took a sip of her coffee, but her gaze never wavered from Celia's across the table.

A blush heated her face at the mere mention of the night before. Mason had been insatiable. Almost as insatiable as her. They'd barely managed to get their clothes back on in time for Mrs. Chambers to spring them from the basement. "Wh-what do you mean?"

"The party. For Price and me." Aubrey tucked a stray lock of her long, dark hair behind her ear and spoke slowly, as if to a mentally challenged child. "Did you have a good time?"

"Oh. Right. The party." Celia's laugh was breathless. "It was great. Good food."

The brunette's lips twitched. "I noticed you left early. You didn't even say good-bye."

"Um. Sorry about that."

She took another sip of her drink. "Price also noted that Mason disappeared around the same time."

Busted.

Stabbing a few pieces of lettuce from her salad, Celia muttered, "You wouldn't believe me if I told you the truth about what happened."

"Oh, *this* I have to hear." Her best friend leaned forward, a grin curling her lips.

Celia sighed and met her eyes. "Jerry and Mrs. Chambers locked us in the basement together."

"What?" Aubrey straightened, shock coloring her voice. "No way!"

"I know, right?" Celia threw her hands into the air, the lettuce leaves on her fork fluttering wildly. She ate them quickly, then continued explaining. "We went down to bring up more champagne for the party and the next thing we know, the door's locked shut. They left us a note saying they'd let us out in the morning."

"Which they did, since you're here."

"Yeah."

"And you got busy with Mason. Finally." Satisfaction rang in her friend's voice.

Jesus, *everyone* had been rooting for her to sex it up with him. Except her. The morning had arrived to bite her in the ass, just as she'd known it would. What had she been thinking? Who was she kidding—she *hadn't* been thinking. The man confused the hell out of her, made her wish for things she didn't believe in anymore. Things she had very good reasons not to believe in. There were no fairy tales, no marriage and white picket fences and ever afters. She pushed her plate away and groaned. "Yeah."

"Was it good?" Aubrey propped her chin in her palm, a wicked smile flashing across her face.

Celia sighed again, letting her head drop to the table. "Yeah."

"Uh, well...that's a bummer." The other woman reached over and patted Celia's shoulder.

She tilted her head to glare out of the corner of her eye. "Shut up."

"Have fun with it." Aubrey shrugged and sat back. She snagged a cherry tomato off her plate and popped it in her mouth. "I did with his brother, and it didn't turn out too badly."

Celia growled and slumped on her stool, folding her arms. "It was a one-time thing. No encore."

Taking a bite of her sandwich, Aubrey spoke around the food in her mouth. "Does he know that?"

"He ran out a few minutes after they sprang us." Celia shrugged, assuring herself that she had *not* been disappointed to see him go. "Got called in to a fire."

Aubrey swallowed and took a swig of her coffee. "I wouldn't be surprised if he comes back for seconds."

Leaning forward, Celia snagged one of the cookies. Moments like this called for food more comforting—and fattening—than a salad. "He had seconds. And thirds."

Choking on her drink, the brunette grabbed a napkin and

laugh-snorted into it. "Oh-ho! Nice."

Celia considered throwing the rest of her cookie at her friend, but decided against punishing the poor food that way. Instead she rolled her eyes. "Shut up."

Her heart did *not* flutter at the suggestion that Mason might want another night with her. Or even more than that.

No. No, no, no, *no*. This was exactly why she hadn't wanted to hook up with him in the first place. She hadn't even been willing to go on a single date with him because she had *known* this would happen. She'd get all schoolgirl twitter-pated, instead of acting like the bitter divorcee she actually was. Stomping down on that sweet quivery feeling in the pit of her stomach, she reminded herself that she was just a challenge that Mason had overcome. He'd gotten what he'd wanted.

End of story. No happy ending.

As usual.

After she finished up her last appointment at the salon, she closed up shop and went around to the staircase on the side of the building that led to her apartment on the second floor. A few minutes later, she stood in front of her freezer, deciding between microwavable pizza and a TV dinner when her doorbell rang. Closing the refrigerator, she jogged toward the door. Her heart leapt when she saw a tall male shape outlined through the frosted glass that made up the top half of her front door. Still, she called, "Who is it?"

"Mason."

Just as she'd suspected.

Heat raced up her face, then sluiced back down again until every inch of her skin felt warm and tingly. She swallowed, trying to come up with something intelligent to say other than *do me, baby...again.*

"It's too late to pretend you're not there, Celia." His voice sounded amused rather than impatient, which made her want to smile, and that made her angry with herself...and with him. He shouldn't be able to affect her so much just with the tone of his voice.

She yanked open the door and scowled. "Isn't this a new level of desperation and harassment for you? I thought you were showing your versatility by not pursuing me anymore."

"I'm not pursuing." His hands were tucked behind his back, and he favored her with a slow grin. "I already had you. Now I'm keeping, not pursuing."

"You don't have me to keep. We had sex."

"I know." He ran his gaze over her in a slow, thorough fashion. It made her body and her temper heat up even more. "I was there."

"What do you want, Mason? I'm busy." She folded her arms over her chest to hide her tightening nipples. Just a look from him made her react. Damn it.

He moved his hands around for her to see. "I brought dinner. You just finished at the salon, so I know you haven't eaten yet."

"Stalker."

His grin widened, obviously enjoying that he got to her. "That's very flattering, honey."

"I'm not your honey," she grumbled, squeezing her thighs together to suppress the ache between them. She'd had more sex last night than she'd had in months. She should be more than satisfied, not lubing up for another round. Considering how little sleep she'd had, her body should be ready to drop from exhaustion, not humming with anticipation.

"You didn't protest last night."

Yeah, like she needed a reminder. Her stomach rumbled,

reminding her that she'd been trying to figure out what to eat before he'd arrived. The way she figured it, she had a choice here. She could stand there and argue with him until she died of starvation, or she could take him up on dinner. There were definite pros and cons to both options. Another hungry grinding in her belly decided for her. "Shut up and give me the food before it gets cold."

He held it just beyond her reach. "I brought it to *share*. This isn't a delivery service."

"And here I was hoping for *full service* delivery," she purred in her most sex kitten voice, just to yank his chain.

His mouth flapped open, but no words came forth.

She grinned, snatched the bag from him and left him standing in the doorway. Darting into her kitchen, she set the paper sack on the counter and pulled out several Styrofoam cartons. "Mmm...this is from the restaurant next door."

"You haven't even opened the containers." He closed the door behind him and wandered around her living room, not touching anything, but taking everything in.

"Please, it's next door. You think I don't know that smell?" She tried not to feel uncomfortable and exposed with him in her space, looking around, assessing it. Assessing her. She hadn't thought about that when she'd let him in. She should have. Busying herself with dishing up the food onto plates, she tried to ignore how he managed to shrink the place down with his presence.

"The waitress knew what you liked." He settled himself on one of the stools at her counter.

"I may have been there once or twice. A week." She chuckled, set a plate in front of him, and went back to pour them each a glass of sparkling water. She had wine, but she figured adding alcohol to their mix was a bad idea. "They might know me."

"Not a big cook?" He stood and pulled out a stool for her to sit. She put the glasses on the counter while he grabbed her food and brought it to her. He resumed his seat beside her, his shoulder and thigh brushing hers.

She swallowed a whimper and concentrated harder than she should have had to on the conversation. "I have time for cooking when, exactly?" She waved a hand to encompass her house. "Plus, I live alone. If I cook, I have to eat the same thing for a week."

"I know what you mean." He saluted her with his glass. "I've lived alone for a couple of years now."

And before that, he'd have lived with his last fiancée. A twist of jealousy she absolutely refused to acknowledge wrenched through her. They'd had a one-night stand, nothing more. There was no reason for her to be envious. None. They'd never even been out on a date, and that was entirely her choice. She didn't date anymore. So there. No jealousy and that was final. She snorted at that stupidity, but what else could she do?

What she wanted to ask him was why he was even here in the first place. They'd had sex, they both knew he didn't do commitment, so last night had to be the perfect arrangement for him. What was he still sniffing around here for? And why did she care anyway?

As usual, she didn't know if she was coming or going with him. Damn. It. So, she did the only thing she could—she plied herself to her food while he did the same. The silence was more companionable than she would have expected, and after a while, she relaxed and enjoyed her dinner. The waitress had sent her favorite pasta primavera dish, and the meal hit the spot. So much better than the frozen dinner she'd been considering.

"You know..." He cast her a sidelong glance. "We're eating dinner together."

"Uh...yeah. You did bring the food." She arched her eyebrows and gave him the kind of pitying look reserved for simpletons.

He ignored her sarcasm. "This could almost count as a date."

Yeah, like she was buying that line of crap. "This is no more a date than when I ate lunch with Aubrey this afternoon. I share food with a lot of people. That doesn't mean I'm dating them all. In fact, I don't date. Period."

"*Never?*" His expression couldn't have been more horrified than if she announced she had an STD. A deathly contagious one at that.

She couldn't help it. She laughed in his face. "Not since the last divorce, no."

"And how long ago was that?"

"A few years." It surprised her that she had to think about it. "It's not like I don't have a life outside of dating. I'm not sitting around singing *Someday My Prince Will Come.*"

"As long as the prince gets to come inside you, I'll be your Prince Charming." His grin was sin incarnate.

Reaching over, she poked him with her fork and made him jolt. "There is no Prince Charming. That's the point. Why date when I know there's not going to be that marriage and happy-ever-after ending? It's pointless."

"So, if you don't date, how do you..." He trailed off as if he had no idea how to ask the question.

"You mean, aside from my vibrator?" Her shoulder dipped in a shrug. "I have my go-to guys and that's it. No strings, no recriminations, no planning for some fake future. Just sex. Which is all we had last night. We are not *dating.*" She made the word a dirty, vile thing.

He snorted and rubbed a hand over his shorn hair. "You

know, a few weeks ago, I'd have been happy to hear you wanted a sex-only arrangement."

"Oh, yeah? What changed?" Not that she cared why he might not be satisfied with sex-only. She totally didn't. Not in the least. She was just making conversation. It was polite.

Pushing his empty plate away, he sighed. "If you can believe it, I had an interesting conversation with Mrs. Chambers."

"Yeah?" Her eyebrows arched. Whatever she'd been expecting him to say, that hadn't been it.

He nodded. "About us, actually."

"What about us?" There was an *us* worth talking about with the biggest busybody in Oregon?

He took a swig of his water. "She asked me why I kept asking you out."

"I asked you that all the time." Until he'd stopped asking.

"Yeah, this was right before I quit coming around."

"So you didn't just want to show me your versatility?"

He chuckled, the sound smooth and mellow. "No. It's just...the way she put it made me really stop and think about it. Why *was* I being so stubborn? If a woman isn't interested, she isn't interested. No harm, no foul. If I want a date or want to get laid, I don't have to beg for it."

Well, he wasn't lying about that. Everyone in town thought she was an idiot for turning him down. A million times. Most of the single women would bang him in a heart beat. Some of the married ones too.

He tapped his fingers on the countertop. "I haven't done a real relationship since my last engagement ended. I never thought I'd want to. Some casual dating, sex, sure. Commitment and all the baggage that goes with it, no."

"I can understand that." Her reasoning was pretty similar,

if a little more extreme. Then again, divorce was a hell of a lot worse than ending an engagement. There were lawyers involved. She huffed out a laugh. "It's funny, when we first met and you first asked me out, I told Aubrey you were the marrying kind and I wasn't going down that road—or aisle—again. But then...well, you made it clear you were the hit it and quit it type, so I guess I was wrong."

"No, you weren't." His voice was so quiet, she wouldn't have heard him if she weren't sitting right next to him.

"Oooo-kay." Her heart tripped, and she didn't know what else to say.

He turned on his stool to face her, his green eyes daring her to look away. "See, I've been telling myself all along, it was just because I wanted to get you in bed with me. Once I got you out of my system, I'd be fine."

"Nice." She rolled her eyes.

One broad shoulder hunched in a shrug. "It's not nice. It's just the truth."

"Fair enough."

"But then I have to go back to, why you? Why did I have to get *you* in bed with me? Why would I keep asking for a year? And that's where I hit a wall." He rubbed a finger over the bridge of his nose. "Mrs. Chambers made me finally figure it out."

"Oh, this is going to be interesting." She forked up a last piece of pasta and licked her lips. "Okay, I'll bite. Why me?"

His gaze went to her mouth, and she saw the banked fire in his eyes. "Because I *want* a relationship with you. I don't want to sleep with you and get you out of my system. I don't want to get you out of my system, period." He swallowed. "I've spent the last few weeks working through some personal shit—"

"What personal shit, exactly?" She interrupted him, hoping to divert him from any more talk of relationships and offering

162

himself up as her fairy tale prince.

"Mrs. C told me you'd been married twice, and from what you've said, she let you know I've been engaged to three different women." He held up three fingers to emphasize his point.

"Never managed to close the deal, huh?" Mock sympathy filled her tone and she patted his leg. She realized how close she was to certain parts of his anatomy, and yanked her hand away.

His fingers snapped around her wrist and drew her palm to his lips. He kissed her hand, which made her shiver, then he nipped at the base of her thumb. "Unlike you, I figured out they weren't right for me before we took that walk down the aisle."

"Touché." She grinned and tugged her arm from his grasp, rubbing her fingertips over the spots his mouth had touched. "You broke it off all three times?"

"Nah." He ran a hand down his chin. "I ended it with first one, which was a relief for her, I think. We were too young. She was my high school sweetheart, and I thought I wanted to spend my life with her, but we had a lot of growing up to do. We were both in college and we just...became different people." His grin turned rueful. "The second one left me."

Despite herself, Celia was interested. Fascinated, was more like it. She'd spent the last year loaded down with uncertainty when it came to him, so learning more was probably something she should avoid, but she was too curious not to listen. "She's the one who didn't like the firefighter schedule?"

"Among other things." He propped his elbow on the counter and sighed. "She didn't like the danger of my job, didn't like that I could be called in for an emergency at any time, so making plans could be problematic. We both thought she could adjust, but...no. I guess I should have seen it coming when she walked, but the truth is it kicked me in the gut."

Linking her fingers together, she managed not to reach out to him. The echo of pain in his voice was something she could relate to. She cleared her throat. "And the third fiancée?"

"She was the firefighter." He swallowed and glanced away, but not before she saw the flash of devastation. If the second fiancée had hurt him, it was nothing compared to this one. He let out a slow breath. "She died on the job."

Her chest cinched tight, and this time she couldn't stop herself from squeezing his hand in sympathy. "I'm so sorry."

"I stayed in L.A. for a few years after it happened, but going into the firehouse every time just...hurt." His fingers gripped hers a little too tight, and his focus turned inward. Shaking his head, his voice went rough. "I couldn't stop thinking about it, and I knew that wasn't healthy. Hell, I didn't even realize *how* bad off I was until an old friend tapped me to take a job in Cedarville. He dragged me up to check it out. It was fucking amazing. The further away from home I got, the better I felt. It was like a huge weight lifted off my chest, and after three years, I could suddenly *breathe* again." He ran his free hand over the back of his neck. "Never looked back."

She groped for something else to talk about, to take his mind off the ugliness. "It's nice that Price followed you here."

A soft laugh straggled out of him and he released her hand. "Yeah, I like having him around. He's a good brother. "

"It must have been nice having a sibling. I always wished I'd had one." Someone to share her painful losses with might have kept her from making some of the dumbest mistakes of her life, such as marriage number one and number two. Then again, her life had made her who she was and she was okay with that. She liked herself and she'd accepted her mistakes as part of living.

"Yeah, I figure if I ever have kids, I'd want at least two." He chuckled. "Siblings can be a pain in the ass, but they can also be a blessing."

"You want kids?" Somehow, that hadn't occurred to her. He seemed like such a *guy*, and wishing for babies just didn't fit the picture of him she had in her head. Then again, she'd never have guessed he was carrying around the kind of past he had. The three failed engagements had always made her see the *love 'em and leave 'em* type when she looked at him, but now she wasn't so sure.

"Someday, maybe." His smile turned self-deprecating. "I sort of planned on it during...well, *all three* of my engagements. What about you?"

"Um, I don't know." She glanced away and shrugged. Somehow, they had drifted to dangerous territory again. No way was she discussing her future kids with him. "My divorces haven't really meant good marriages and happy families. I always figured if it happened, it happened."

"No planning for you, huh?" His gaze searched her face for a long moment, but she had no clue what he might be looking for. "Anyway. I've spent the last few weeks sorting through all that old baggage, so I get it if you still need some time, but this relationship *is* going to happen. How amazing last night was just makes me even more determined to keep you."

There didn't seem to be any derailing him. Hopelessness punched through her. She'd had a hard enough time resisting him when he'd just wanted a date, but if he started pushing for more? After the emotional high of the night before and now that she knew more about what he'd been through? No. God, no. She firmed her jaw. "No one keeps me—everyone leaves. That's just how it is. I don't *do* relationships. Not anymore. I do light, casual sex. No strings attached."

"That's fine. We can start there." His answer was immediate, his tone far too easy, and she suspected he'd had this part of his little speech planned before he'd shown up with dinner. "I'm going to try and change your mind, but I'm not stupid enough to turn down sex with you after having a semi for the last year anytime you were near me."

A half-laugh burst out of her. "That's really romantic."

"I'm not really romantic." He lifted his hands in the air. "Never have been, never will be. But I'll treat you right, even if it's not all candlelit dinners and walks on the beach."

"It was *just* sex." Her voice was just a little bit too desperate. Was she trying to convince him, or herself? This was why she should never have given in to temptation. And now she was being punished.

"Okay." He smiled. "For now."

"You're obnoxious." She gripped the edge of the counter and stared down at the gleaming granite surface. "And I never said I was sleeping with you again. One night was enough for me."

A bolt of lightning was going to strike her any second for telling that whopper, she just knew it, but if she didn't look Mason in the eyes, he might not be able to see the lie for what it was. Awareness hummed through her body and had since he'd walked in the door. She wished she could shut it off, but she'd been failing at that since the day they'd met.

He leaned in until she could feel his warm breath brush the side of her neck. "You didn't enjoy yourself?"

Clenching her fingers on the counter, she refused to give in to the wave of molten fire that coursed through her at his nearness. "You know I did."

"But you don't want to enjoy yourself like that again?" His lips grazed her throat and tingles exploded down her skin. She fought a shudder and could do nothing about the way her nipples contracted.

Her breath rushed out, but she couldn't form a single thought enough to say anything. His hand covered hers, stroking her tense fingers and up her arm. Goosebumps broke out across her skin, and it took everything in her to keep from throwing herself at him. There wasn't a hope in hell of pushing him away. Now that she'd had him, she only wanted more.

"There's nothing I can do to force you into a relationship, right?" He ran his tongue up her neck to her ear, then blew a cool breath along the moisture he'd left behind. "I can try to change your mind, but I can't *make* you. Right?"

"Right." Her voice came out weaker than she would have liked, but at least she'd managed to squeak the word out. She wanted to rub herself against him, feel that exquisite friction again.

"So you have nothing to lose, and you get some great sex in the bargain. This can't go any further than you allow it to." He captured her earlobe and worried it between his teeth. At the same time, his fingers moved to stroke the sensitive underside of her breast.

The dual assault broke her. "We are *not* dating. There will be no relationship. We're just having sex."

It was the last bit of sanity and self-preservation she could muster before she turned into his embrace. Groaning, he stood and pulled her off the stool. One of his hands twined in her hair, holding her in place. The other hand roamed her back, her bottom, making her whimper and squirm to get closer. Just like the night before, the second he touched her she went up in flames. Her heart pounded in her chest, her blood rushing madly through her veins.

She tugged on his shirt, pulling it out of his pants so that she could get her hands under it. His skin was rough velvet under her palms—smooth hot skin and crisp curly hair. Skating her fingertips over his chest, she found his small nipples and circled then. His hips jerked and he moaned, his hands tightening almost painfully on her backside, but he didn't stop her. She smiled against his mouth and teased his nipples until they beaded into hard little points.

167

He moved his hands around until he could unfasten her pants, dipping his fingers inside to stroke her through her panties. Shock hit her, and she jolted, pinching his nipple hard in reflex. A sound that was somewhere between a chuckle and a groan erupted from him. He broke their kiss, shoving her slacks down her legs. She kicked aside her shoes and stepped out of her pants, letting him pull her top off.

"Take your clothes off too." She pushed his shirt up, wanting all of him naked. Now.

Instead of listening to her, he leaned back to take in her undergarments. "Were you expecting me?"

"Nope." A grin quirked one corner of her lips. Today she had on scraps of fire engine red silk and lace. "I always wear nice undies. It makes me feel sexy."

"You're always sexy, no matter what you're wearing. But if I'd known all this time that you had *this* kind of thing on under your clothes every time I saw you…" He groaned, not bothering to finish the sentence as he swooped down to draw her nipple into his mouth, sucking the tight tip through the lace of her bra.

Pleasure exploded inside her, and she held onto his shoulders for balance. "More, please. *More.*"

He switched to her other breast, sucked the crest deep into his mouth and bit down. Batting the imprisoned nipple with his tongue rubbed the lace over her sensitized flesh, and a sound of utter need erupted from her throat. Her sex clenched on nothingness, and she could feel herself dancing on the ragged edge of orgasm. She shoved away from him, her chest heaving with each breath.

Eyes glazed, he swayed toward her, his hands twitching as though he might reach for her again. "Did I hurt you? Are you all right?"

"Bed. Now." That was the most lucidity she could hope for

at the moment. She turned and walked toward her bedroom, his heavy tread following her down the short hallway. Her thighs brushed together with each step, making her aware of how little she was wearing, and her excitement ratcheted up by the second.

Thankfully, her room was relatively tidy, with only her clothes from the night before strewn across the mattress. Though at this point, she wouldn't care if the place were a sty. He hooked her discarded bra up with a finger. "Mmm. I have fond memories of this little number."

"Get naked, Delacroix." She scooped everything off the bed and onto the floor, then she stripped out of her undergarments.

He chuckled, but yanked his shirt over his head and toed his shoes off at the same time. She reached for his belt, unbuckling it. Anything to speed this process up. Her heart raced, beads of sweat already gathering at her temples. Unfastening his fly, she pushed his pants and boxers down until they hit the floor.

His cock sprang free of the restraints and she cupped him in her palms, stroking up and down his erection. He was long and thick, so big that she wasn't sure how she'd taken him the night before, but she knew she wanted to try again. She also wanted to taste him. Taking a step back, she perched on the side of her bed, which put her mouth on the same level as his dick. A pearl of fluid trailed down from the tip of his shaft, and she traced its path with her nail.

He shuddered, his hips following the motion of her hand. "Don't tease me, sweetheart."

Figuring actions spoke louder than words, she darted her tongue out to lick the bulbous crest. His fingers splayed against the back of her head, urging her closer. Circling her fingers around his cock, she squeezed tight and pumped him hard, once, twice. He swore under his breath when she sucked him into her mouth. She slid down on him until he touched the back of her throat, running her tongue along the underside of his cock. The muskiness of his skin made her moan, and his hand fisted in her hair when the vibrations hit his shaft.

"I'm going to come if you keep that up."

She giggled, suckling him harder for a moment before letting him slide free of her mouth. "Well, we can't have that. Yet."

"Brat." He sat beside her on the edge of the mattress, and before she could blink, he'd hauled her facedown on his lap. His warm palm cupped her backside. "I think that deserves a little retribution, don't you?"

Anticipation swamped her. Her heart jolted, her pulse leaping into a gallop. Oh, God. This was something she hadn't tried before, but she couldn't deny that the concept made cream flood her pussy. "O-okay."

"*Reeeally*?" He drew the word out, making it sound wicked, sensual. Dangerous.

The upturned position made all the blood rush to her face. He stroked the tips of his fingers over the globes of her ass, then scraped his blunt nails across her flesh. It hurt, just a little. Just enough to whet her appetite. She swallowed, excitement a living thing within her.

He drew back and slapped her buttocks one at a time. The sting of it made her jump, made her shudder with lust that wouldn't be quelled. The next swats were harder, and she arched her ass into his touch. The pleasure-pain was like nothing she'd ever experienced before. It was titillating and overwhelming and erotic as hell.

Dragging his nails down her skin this time had her hissing in a breath. He dipped between her thighs, plunging his fingers into her pussy. She screamed, bucking her hips to take him deeper. He worked her sex hard, then trailed her moisture up to ease his passage into her anus. She choked as his fingertip penetrated her ass, whimpered when he moved back to her sex and repeated the process again and again until he could press two big digits into her backside. He growled in satisfaction, scissoring his fingers to widen her further. "I'm going to fuck you here."

"*Yes.*" Tingles broke down her limbs, and she could feel orgasm gathering inside her. Her muscles tightened, belly quivering as the sensations rocketed through her.

So close. She was so close.

He stopped toying with her and resumed spanking her. The shock was almost more than she could bear, but did little to cool her ardor. Her whole being centered on where his hand would land next, and each slap made her skin hotter, her sex wetter. Throughout it all, she could feel the rigid length of his cock pulsing against her bare hip.

Twisting in his lap, she clutched at the bedspread and rode out the agony as her pussy contracted with each smack. Her control snapped. "Stop, Mason!"

He froze, his body stilling, his heaving breath loud in the sudden silence. An edge of worried panic in his voice, he demanded, "Are you all right?"

"No more," she gasped. "I can't take it. I want you inside me."

"Thank God." He sagged in relief.

Slithering off his lap, she knelt on the bed beside him, her body throbbing. She nipped at his shoulder with her teeth. "*Now*, Mason."

"Yes. Now." He leaned over and swiped his pants off the floor, fishing a condom out of one pocket.

He rolled to his back, and she straddled his thighs while he sheathed himself in the condom. He pulled her in place over his cock, his fingers biting into her flesh, but he let her set the pace. She rolled her hips, rubbing her wet folds against the

171

head of his dick. A muscle bulged in his jaw, and he made a choked sound, shuddering beneath her. She took him slowly, though her body screamed for more, harder and faster and now, but she wanted to savor this moment.

Sinking down on his thick shaft one slow inch at a time, she let her head fall back as she lost herself in the feel of his cock stretching her. It was fucking amazing. Better than anything she'd ever known before. She gasped when he arched beneath her, rocking his pelvis against her clit. The head of his cock hit her G-spot, and she screamed. *"Jesus Christ."*

"I can't wait, Celia. I need you." He gritted the words out between clenched teeth. "Fuck me, ride me hard. Please."

She gave him what he wanted, planting her hands on his shoulders for leverage as she began pumping her hips. The fit was perfect. She was so full. Sweat slipped down her skin, and she shivered. Too many sensations, too much to take in at once. But there was no other option except to take it all, because she couldn't have stopped moving if her life depended on it. She lifted and lowered herself on his cock, faster and faster, needing that carnal friction, loving the sound of their moans, the slap of skin against skin, the creak of the mattress underneath them.

Her sex fisted every time she took him deep inside, and she sobbed for breath. Sliding his hand between them, he thumbed her clit. "Come for me, Celia."

There was no choice. She imploded, her pussy pulsing around his cock. He dragged it out for her, kept her hips surging to meet his touch on her clitoris. She dug her nails into his shoulders as she catapulted over another peak, her sex contracting so hard that stars burst behind her eyelids.

She collapsed against him, panting. It took her a few moments to resurface enough to notice the tension running through him, and that he was still thick and hard inside her. That didn't make sense, and she shook her head to try and clear it. Blinking blurry eyes, she looked up at him. "You didn't come?"

"I didn't want it to be over yet." His smile was a little strained and a lot wicked. "I promised to fuck your ass, remember?"

A vivid image formed in her mind of exactly what he described. His big cock, sliding into her stretched anus. Her mouth dried, and just that fast, she was hot and ready again. Her hips rolled a bit, and he groaned. She dropped her forehead to his sweat-dampened shoulder. "There's a bottle of lube in the bedside table."

"Oh, yeah?"

"I like to use it occasionally...when I self-entertain." At least, that was the only use this bottle had been put to. It really *had* been a while since she'd let a man into her bed.

He made a small, choked sound. "I would love to watch you some time...when you self-entertain."

A shiver passed through her at the thought. God, he was naughty. And she liked that about him. "One thing at a time."

"Yeah...I want to take my time with you." His tone added extra meaning to his words, which she chose to ignore. This was not the right moment to argue about their not-going-to-happen future relationship.

She had other ideas in mind.

Climbing off of him, she moaned when his cock slid out of her pussy. She crawled over to the side of the mattress, tugged out the drawer to her nightstand and fished around until she came up with the clear container of lube.

One of his palms slid down her back to cup her sore buttocks. The other hand plucked the lube from her grasp. "I'll take that."

Her arms shook as exhilaration twisted inside her. She

closed her eyes and drew in a shuddery breath when he popped open the top of the bottle. His hand continued to stroke over her spanked backside, making tingles break down her skin. Cold lube slid into the crack of her ass, and she squealed, jerking forward, but there was nowhere to go. She was already at the edge of the bed. "You could have warmed it up. Damn it!"

He chuckled, his palm smacking her butt lightly. "Where's the fun in that? I like making you react."

"I'm noticing that," she grumbled, wriggling her hips while the lube warmed against her skin. "You better make this up to me."

He dropped a kiss on her backside. "I will. I promise."

Parting her buttocks, he pressed his fingers to her anus, sliding the liquid into her. She clenched her hands in the sheets, her back bowing at the intensity of the stretch when he added a second, then a third digit. Her breath panted out, sweat slipping down her skin. Closing her eyes, she focused on the sheer visceral experience. All her other senses intensified until her entire world narrowed down to the scent of sex and Mason filling her nose, the sound of their heaving lungs, the rush of her heartbeat thrumming in her ears, the caress of the smooth sheets under her hands and knees, the feel of his fingers moving over her and in her.

A cry burst from her throat when he pulled away from her, some distant part of her mind uncertain how she'd survive if he left her now, but his voice was a soothing rumble. "Shh... I'm not going anywhere, sweetheart. We're just getting started."

The head of his dick nudged at her anus, piercing the ring of muscle and filling her ass. Slowly. Oh, so slowly. It was agony to wait when her body screeched for more, for the satisfaction he could give her. She pushed her hips back, but his hands fitted around her waist, holding tight and not letting her take more of him. They were going at his speed and no faster. She moaned and clamped her inner muscles tight around his thick

174

shaft. "Hurry."

He hissed out a breath, and she felt a shudder run through him.

"I don't want to hurt you, baby." The words were rough and uneven, like his breathing.

When he was all the way in her, he stayed there for what seemed like forever. There was no pain, just incredible pressure and pleasure as he stimulated her nerve endings. Rocking her ass into his pelvis made them both groan. She wanted a swift drive toward orgasm.

He withdrew in the same unhurried pace with which he'd entered her, and she thought the anticipation punching through her might send her reeling into madness if he didn't *go faster*. Harder. Deeper. Right this very second.

"Mason, I am going to hurt *you* if you don't move your ass." She shot him a glare over her shoulder.

A sinful grin creased his cheeks. "Like this, you mean?"

He arched his hips and plunged into her ass, giving her exactly what she'd asked for. On his next thrust, she pushed back to meet him. She whimpered as his stomach smacked against her aching buttocks. That same lash of white-hot ecstasy whipped through her, pain and pleasure and something far deeper that she didn't even want to examine. Her heart squeezed, but she shoved away any burgeoning emotions. This was sex, nothing more. This was all she would allow. The only happy endings there were happened at the end of a good shag.

Holding on to the mindless release he offered her, she worked her body in time with his and refused to think about anything else. Just this. Just him. Nothing else existed. No past, no future, just this moment.

He filled her ass again, swifter and rougher, using his hold on her waist to pull her back into his strokes, forcing his cock as deep as it would go. Her lungs burned as she moved with him, unable to go fast enough to satisfy herself. It was so good. The best she'd ever known, and even admitting that much was dangerous. She shifted her weight and reached down to fondle her clit in time to his thrusts. He pistoned in and out of her anus, and she moaned with each penetration. Her internal muscles contracted, and the orgasm she craved shimmered at the edge of her consciousness, beckoning her to lose all control. She threw herself toward it, shoving her fingers into her pussy and letting the heel of her hand grind against her clit as Mason ground his pelvis against her ass.

Release broke through her, and she screamed. Her pussy flexed around her fingers, and she could feel his cock moving in her ass through the thin layer of flesh that separated her two channels. His grip on her waist became almost painful, and she could tell how close he was to orgasm by the ragged edge to his breathing. He groaned, shuddering over her as he came as well. After a long moment, he pulled out of her.

She tumbled sideways, sprawling on the mattress. Well, she'd gotten her wish. There wasn't a single thought in her head. Bliss buzzed through her system, and she sighed.

"We're pretty damn good at this." Mason collapsed beside her, his hand cupping the back of her thigh.

"Mmm-hmm."

"Imagine how good we'd be with a lot of practice." His fingers brushed over her skin, trailing up to the sensitized flesh of her backside. She could still feel the heat of his spanking, and goose bumps erupted down her arms and legs. "Years of practice."

She stirred, frowning as what he'd said pierced her bubble of contentment. "I think we're doing fine now. We've both had previous practice."

"Yeah, but tell me it was as good as this."

It would have been easy to shut him down right then and

there, but a lie that huge refused to cross her lips. So, instead of giving him what he wanted, she remained silent.

"Of course, it wasn't." He continued stroking her skin, his voice as gentle as his touch. "Chemistry like this doesn't just come around every day. And you've had *previous practice*, so you know that already."

He was right, and she hated it. "So?"

If she sounded disgruntled, she didn't give a damn. He'd gone and killed her post-coital glow, and she wasn't going to pretend she was happy about it.

"So, imagine having this every day. Any time you wanted." His voice dropped to a low purr, and he turned his head to look at her.

"Until everything else turns to crap, and the relationship implodes, and we end up hating each other." Even though she knew it was true, it still depressed the shit out of her. She closed her eyes and sighed.

"It doesn't have to be that way." His tone turned cajoling, convincing, and she hated herself for *wanting* to believe him.

"Has it ever turned out better than that for you before? Of course not, or you wouldn't be single. I prefer to enjoy this moment right here and not weigh it down with all kinds of worry about which way it has to be or should be. Let's just leave it at that and not push." She looked at him again, snared by the compelling light in his green eyes. How he could have any hope left after three broken engagements, she didn't know, and she wasn't going to ask. Encouraging him to talk about this would be a stupid thing to do.

"You have to admit though." He grinned at her. "That. Was. *Awesome.*"

She laughed, the serious moment passing, and she was grateful. She had a feeling he'd broken the tension on purpose, giving her an out because he knew she couldn't take more. It was surprising, considerate. Not what she'd expect from such a forceful personality.

"Yeah, it was awesome."

Chapter Four

The man had the persistence of a rabid terrier. Celia growled and swept up a few stray locks of hair around her cutting chair.

Over the last few weeks, Mason had gotten around her no dating rule by making a habit of showing up at her salon just before closing time. He was also annoyingly good at making himself useful. He'd rewired a dryer that liked to stop for no apparent reason, fixed a clogged sink and generally made her stylists love having him around. When they finished up for the day, he happened to be there to take her to dinner or to talk her into feeding him. It didn't really matter which option they went with, he inevitably pulled her close, kissed her, stroked his hands over her body. And she was lost. He ended up in her bed every night he wasn't working at the firehouse.

Which meant that he was due to show up any time, but she'd found a good excuse not to dine with him tonight. She was going to have to cut this off soon, and she ignored the way that depressed her. She sighed and set the broom aside, glancing around at the two other stylists who were cleaning up for the night. Then her gaze took in the rest of the salon, making sure everything was in place. It was, and it looked great—just the way she wanted it. She'd renovated when she'd purchased the building, retaining the feel of the old barbershop inside like she had outside, while updating to the sleek standards of a modern salon. The result was a little bit country, a little bit rock and roll—perfect for Celia.

The bell over the door jingled, and she didn't even have to turn around to know it was Mason. After three weeks, her body was attuned to him. She glanced back and her heart turned over at the little smile that softened the sharp angles of his face. He only used that look on her, and she refused to let herself consider what that might mean. He was not going to win this campaign of his. She knew better than to go down that road again. If she had to remind herself—and him—of that on a regular basis, then that was how it was going to be. She should just cut her losses and run, but she hadn't been able to do it. Yet. She was enjoying this thing with him too much to walk away. She would, she had to, but not now. It was a stupid, dangerous game she was playing with her own heart, but she couldn't make herself stop yet.

He stepped up behind her, closing his hands over her shoulders and kneading out any tension from being on her feet all day. She moaned, her head dropping forward. He kissed the nape of her neck. "Hey, you're closed Sundays and Mondays, and that's where my days off fall this week, so let's do something. Go to the coast and spend the day on the beach."

"Nope." She pulled away from him, though she didn't want to. It sounded like a great time, but with a man like Mason, if she gave an inch, he'd take a mile. Or ten.

Picking her purse up from the counter in front of her chair, she caught him watching her in the mirror. He narrowed his gaze at her, assessing, looking for chinks in her armor. "Fine, no beach. I'm taking you next door for dinner right now."

"But..."

He folded his arms, arching one dark brow. "Tell me you have plans. Don't stop and think about it, be honest."

"I have plans," she retorted defiantly.

Suspicion filled his expression. "What are they?"

"I'm going to eat at Aubrey's." She'd invited herself over in order to avoid just this situation with Mason. He'd done this to her before...if she didn't have a ready excuse to avoid him, he managed to get his way.

Irritation, frustration and calculation flipped rapidly across his face. Then he grinned. "Okay, I'll go with you. I'm sure Price wouldn't mind some family time."

"Shit." The urge to stomp her foot and launch a hairdryer at his head was almost irresistible. There was no getting around him. If her hormones didn't do her in, he did. There were only so many fronts she could fight on.

Another growl erupted from her, and she spun for the door. "Jerry, can you lock up for the night?"

"Sure thing, sugar lips," he sang out from the back of the salon, a note of glee in his voice. Of course he was happy. Mason had won round seventy-five of this game between them. At this point, *all* of her stylists were rooting against her.

They had a great time at dinner, of course. Aubrey showed off her skills as a chef, and the food was amazing. Seeing Mason with his brother was endearing. They told hilarious stories of their upbringing in Los Angeles, and it was another facet of his personality falling into place. Celia shouldn't like it, but she did. She couldn't have asked for a better evening, until Mason insisted on walking her home since it was after dark. Her protests were shut down by Price—there was no arguing safety with the chief of police.

Once Mason had her to himself, there was no doubt for either of them how the night would end.

Hours later, they sat propped against her headboard, naked after yet another round of mattress gymnastics. She'd broken out her favorite wine, and he'd run next door to get some dessert. Crumbs were the only reminder of his chocolate silk pie. A moan of utter delight poured from her as she finished the last bite of her blackberry cheesecake.

"The waitress said that was your favorite, but I had no idea *how* much you liked it." He stared at her mouth while she swallowed the creamy sweetness.

"I've told you before, they know me there."

He took their plates and forks to set them on the side table. "I thought I'd just gotten lucky with the first server, but they all seem to know you."

She patted his shoulder. "Welcome to small town, USA. Everyone knows everyone here. Give yourself another couple of years and you'll adjust."

"So, you grew up in Cedarville?"

Now there was an unintentionally loaded question. She shifted on the mattress, the springs squeaking under her. "More or less, yeah."

"More or less?" His gaze rested on her, and she could feel the force of his curiosity, but she didn't tend to talk about her past. Or her future. The present was the part that mattered.

"Yeah." She hunched her shoulder, doing nothing to encourage this line of discussion.

Of course he didn't take the hint. He nudged her arm. "What does that mean, exactly?"

"Why do you want to know?" She turned her head to meet his gaze head-on.

Green eyes narrowed, he studied her face for an uncomfortably long moment. "Because I want to know you."

"All I'm willing to offer is sex, so that seems like a bad idea. I try not to borrow trouble." Because it was going to turn up eventually, so why go looking for it? She'd rather not. "Apparently, I need to remind you—again—that *we are not dating.*"

"What, you've never had a *friend* with benefits? It might surprise you how fun it can be—we could end up somewhere good even if neither of us gets exactly what we want."

"Oh." How sad was it that she hadn't even considered that

option? When was the last time she'd been surprised by something *good*? She couldn't remember. She had things she'd worked her ass off for, but a nice gift from fate? Maybe never.

Letting a few beats of silence pass, he continued the conversation. "So...you sort of grew up in Cedarville, but not really? People here talk about you as if you'd been here your whole life."

"Hardly." She sighed, plucking at the edge of a pillowcase and debating whether she should tell him anything about her life. It would open the door for something she'd been trying to avoid for weeks—hell, the last *year*. Letting him in, even a little, was a scary thought. Then again, he could ask just about anyone in Cedarville and they'd tell him anything he wanted to know. They did know her here, her past, but as she'd told him, such was life in a small town. "I stayed here with my aunt Grace during the summers. My mom passed away when I was fifteen, so I moved here and finished high school."

"No dad?"

"He took off when I was about six." She shrugged, a short laugh spilling out of her. "What can I say? Bad taste in men runs in the family. Aunt Grace was married five times, mom had just dumped number four before she died, and I've been hitched twice. Unfortunately."

"What happened?" There was no judgment in his voice, no demand, which was the only reason she was willing to answer.

"The first one was my fault. After my mom passed, I went a little rebellious. My aunt was good to me, but she was strict and I didn't want to listen to anyone or follow anyone's rules." She took a sip of her wine, letting the mellowness of it roll over her tongue. With any luck, it would take the edge off of the pain slicing through her. "I hooked up with the town bad boy, we eloped to Seattle, and three years later, he still wanted the sex, drugs and rock and roll lifestyle. I was too young and stupid to know what I wanted, but I knew it wasn't that. So, I dumped him and enrolled in a community college for business and cosmetology." That had been a rough time in her life. She'd stumbled through figuring out who she was, and she had the emotional scars to prove it. Her heart wrenched even thinking about it. "I worked my ass off, but it was the first time since my mom died that I felt like I wasn't completely...lost."

"I'm sorry."

Just that. No outpouring of sympathy or censure because she'd been a dumb kid. It was comforting, and her chest warmed.

She offered him a lopsided smile. "Thanks. It was a long time ago."

"His loss." He reached over and ran a comforting hand down her shoulder. A shiver went through her, half in longing for his empathy and half in utter awareness of him as a man. "I bet he's still smoking pot and strumming his guitar."

She laughed, and it felt like it straggled past a weight that had been pressing down on her chest for far too long. When was the last time she'd actually *talked* about this to anyone? Everyone knew about it—secrets were impossible to keep in Cedarville—but no one had ever wanted to discuss it with her. Not that she would have welcomed the topic, because, well, her past wasn't great, so why not focus on what was good? Right now was awesome.

"How did husband number two happen?"

She sighed. "You know, I don't really like to dwell on this stuff."

"I told you about me... I'm just hoping you'll return the favor." He squeezed the back of her neck, letting her fall into silence for long minutes.

"Yeah. Okay." She picked up a pillow and brushed a hand over it, wiping away an invisible crumb. He *had* shared his past with her. It seemed only fair, when he put it that way. "So, I was a stylist in Seattle for about eight years and I was doing really well—"

"What made you come back here?" He jumped on the opening, and she fought back a smile.

She bumped his shoulder with hers. "I'm getting to that, Mr. Pushy."

"Right, sorry." He shot her a quick, self-deprecating grin. "Keep going."

Any urge to smile passed as all the ugly memories came flooding back. She swallowed hard, forcing the words out. "One day I got a call from Aunt Grace. She was sick. Breast cancer. It had already metastasized and spread...everywhere. There was nothing they could do for her except make her comfortable. So, I came back to live with her until the end." Her heart cinched so tight it was all she could do not to cry. Even five years later, it hurt to have lost that old lady. The last of her family. Gone. Her throat closed, saltiness burning at the backs of her eyes. She realized her hands were balled in the pillow, and she consciously relaxed her grip. "It was the least I could do after she took me in as a hellion teen, you know?"

"Yeah." His fingers tangled in her hair, brushing the short strands away from her face.

She cleared her throat, not allowing herself to lean into his touch. But she wanted to. God, she wanted to. "Husband number two was her doctor. I was still grieving over Grace, and he'd been through the end with me. It just seemed natural, easy. We were together for a couple of years, and we were both workaholics. I was trying to get Occam's Razor off the ground and he was a doctor, so we were like ships passing in the night. We never saw each other." Her shoulder twitched in a shrug. "It didn't really surprise me when he left me for one of the nurses at the hospital. It did surprise me how little I cared."

"Ouch."

"Yeah." She braced herself before she turned to look at him. She had no idea what she'd see in his eyes—sympathy or pity or anything in between. Having put this behind her and not talking about it meant she didn't know how other people saw her. Usually, she wouldn't care, but somewhere in the last few weeks, his opinion had become important to her. More important than she'd like to admit. But there was only compassion in his green gaze. Of course, with his past he understood. He continued stroking her hair. His lips were a hairsbreadth from hers, he was so close to her now. "So that was the end of my second marriage."

"I'm sorry." He brushed his mouth over hers, the sweetest kiss she'd ever had. It made that hot moisture burn her eyes again.

She threw herself into his embrace, wanting the comfort that he offered, wanting anything that would distract her from the devastating emotions she'd dredged up. She shouldn't go there, shouldn't give in, because it would only weaken her more in this relationship war they waged, but right then, she couldn't give a flying rat's ass about *shoulds*.

The way he touched her was gentle, as if he feared she might break, as if she were precious to him. Her heart stumbled at the thought, and she wasn't sure if it was in longing or in terror.

He broke his mouth from hers, raining kisses over her face. "Have I told you today how beautiful you are?"

"No." A dart of mischief went through her, and she seized on that instead of all the other things she couldn't handle right now. Avoidance was her friend. "I know something you'd think was even more beautiful."

That made him laugh. "Nothing is more beautiful than you."

"Oh, yeah?" She wiggled out of his arms and moved toward

her dresser, knowing he stared at her ass the entire time, and loving it. He made it clear how much he wanted her, all the time. It was erotic having him watch her, made everything else fade from her mind. Desire swam through her, warmed her body from the inside out. Her nipples gathered into peaks, the lips of her pussy dampening with moisture. Yes, this was how she wanted it. This was how it should be. Not to avoid pain, but just for pleasure.

She pulled something out of her dresser drawer and tossed it to him. His hand snapped out and caught it, then looked down at it. Evil anticipation twisted through her, and she just waited.

After a moment, his entire body froze, then a shudder wracked him. He slowly held up a sheer teddy. "Holy shit."

"My normal lingerie is for myself. *That* kind of thing is for sleepovers." She arched an eyebrow. "Should I get changed for bed?"

As if they hadn't been in bed for hours, but that was entirely beside the point.

"Holy shit," he said again. He looked up at her, his erection rising to impressive proportions, his mouth working for a long moment before he spoke. "So...you think I'll think you're even more beautiful wearing this?"

The dazed look on his face made that wickedness dance through her again. "Yeah, Delacroix, that's the idea. Try to keep up."

He blinked. Blinked again. Shook his head. "I would, but there's no blood left in my brain."

She laughed. "Give it to me."

"I intend to. All night long, if you're in this thing." He held it up by the straps. It had a tie at the neck, in the back and one at each hip. The rest was see-through fishnet. He tossed it to her, crossed his arms, and waited, clearly intent on watching her change into the racy getup.

A flush of heat went through her, half-bashfulness, half-arousal. She set the teddy on the end of the bed—her pulse sped, and she'd never been so aware of a man's gaze moving over her. She pulled the top tie of the teddy over her head, reached behind her to fasten the one in the back, then did the same for those at her hips. A shiver went through her as the fishnet rubbed against her breasts, making her nipples harden to painful points.

Lust whipped through her, liquified her core. The fact that he could see everything through the lingerie made her feel more naked than when she had no clothes on. She offered him the bravest smile she could muster. "All night long, huh? Prove it."

The green fire in his eyes was enough to burn her, but he hesitated. "Are you sure this is what you want tonight?"

She had to respect that he asked, considering what she was wearing and that she could see the rigid proof of his arousal. "I don't want to think about the past, just the now. Distract me, Mason. All night, if you can."

"I can. I will." He grinned then, slow and full of naughty promise. "Come here."

"You come here." Shaking her head, she beckoned to him. He didn't hesitate, rolling to his feet to move toward her.

All those hard muscles bunched and rippled, his cock jutting upward. She loved looking at him. And he looked at her too. His gaze traveled up from her feet to her bare legs. He paused at the thatch of hair between her thighs and lingered on her breasts. She shivered and her breath panted out. White-hot lava flowed through her veins, following in the wake of his gaze.

She was more turned on than she ever had been in her life, and he hadn't even touched her yet.

Dropping to his knees before her, he leaned his forehead against her belly, his palms cupping her hips. "I want you,

188

Celia. I always want you."

"I'm right here," she whispered. "Have me."

"You're here, but for how long?" He tilted his head back and met her gaze.

The open expression made her breathing hitch. She didn't know what to say, what to do. Since her last divorce, she'd run from relationships, and nothing and no one had tempted her the way he had. It was why she'd avoided dating him, knowing instinctively that he'd be a threat to her determination. Her lips trembled when she smiled at him, and she traced her fingertip over his high cheekbone. "I'm here now. That's all I can give you. You've known that from the beginning."

He sighed and closed his eyes. "Yeah. Now I understand why. I just wish..."

So did she. He was the first person to make her wish she were different, that her experiences had been different. But that was fruitless longing. "I'm sorry."

"Don't be." He shook his head and met her gaze again. There was disappointment there that stabbed at her soul. A half-smile kicked up one side of his mouth. "Let's enjoy now, if that's all we get."

Cupping his jaw in her palms, she bent forward to brush his lips with hers, putting everything she couldn't give him into the kiss. It was sweet, hot, everything she'd ever wanted and had found far too late. His tongue pushed into her mouth, and she moaned, the heat she was becoming accustomed to wrenching through her system. His fingers stroked over her hips, tracing the ties that held her lingerie closed.

He released her lips, kissing the lower curve of her stomach through the sheer mesh. She jolted in surprise when he nipped at her belly button. "Mason!"

A rich chuckle was the only answer he gave her. He moved down, dipping his tongue between her thighs to lick her clit.

She gasped when the fishnet material stroked over the tight bundle of nerves, sending an arc of pleasure streaking through her body. The tip of his fingers skimmed the edge of her lingerie, down until he could tease the lips of her pussy.

She pressed her hands to the back of his head, urging him closer. She craved those talented lips on her flesh, wanted him to taste her cream and make her come. His breath rushed over her wet sex, and her muscles quaked in anticipation. He leaned back, tugged the ties at her hips free, and shoved the lower half of her teddy out of his way. He jerked one of her thighs over his shoulder and opened her wide.

Then he buried his face between her legs, feasting on her sex. His fingers stroked up and down her slit while his tongue curled around her clit. A low keen broke from her throat, the intensity of it swamping her. Her pussy flexed on nothingness, and she wanted...she *needed...*

He thrust his fingers deep inside her, and she arched helplessly against him. "Mason, Mason, Mason!"

Climax crashed over her, a flashflood that sent her spinning into oblivion. Her pussy spasmed again and again around his fingers, and a sob wrenched from her. It was too much. Far too much. His tongue and hands continued to work her until her knees buckled.

He caught her, lifting her against his chest. Her heart hammered, and she clutched at his shoulders as he rose to his feet and deposited her on the bed. He came down beside her, sucked her nipples, and the rasp of the mesh with the wet heat of his mouth had her arching off the mattress. Her nails dug into his shoulders, holding him to her. Moans spilled from her throat, her need sharpening once more.

He stripped the rest of her lingerie away, throwing it off the bed. "This is gorgeous, but it's in the way."

"I'm glad you liked it," she gasped.

When she reached out to stroke his cock, he stilled her movements, pressing her hands to the pillow beside her head. "None of that. Tonight is all about you. Just enjoy."

"Okay." She settled back into the mattress, sliding her legs apart. "Don't keep me waiting. I want you inside me."

His laugh was a rough sound of need. "Whatever you want, sweetheart."

He kissed her, and she could taste herself on his lips. The musky scent of sex and him was all she could smell. Their tongues tangled, and her excitement expanded until there was nothing left but desperate, clawing desire. He broke away, his face flushed with lust.

"Condom," he croaked. He rolled away, snagging one from the box they had on the nightstand. Back in seconds, he crawled onto the bed with her and sheathed his cock.

Kneeling between her thighs, he pulled her legs up to drape over his shoulders, turning his head to kiss her ankle. The way he skimmed his fingers down to tease her sex made her twist in reaction. It was unbearable. Her pussy was so wet, she thought she might die if he didn't fill her. "Inside me. Now. Please."

He grasped his cock, rubbing it over her hard clit and slick lips. Raising her hips in offering, she bit back a whimper when he nudged the bulbous crest of his dick into her pussy. The stretch was divine as he eased his wide shaft deep inside her. Groans rolled out of them both as he began moving, and she squeezed her channel around him. He cupped her breasts in his palms, the calluses on his fingers rasping over her nipples. The intense feeling made her grab the sides of the pillow and hold tight, her breath rushing out, her heart thundering in her ears.

A fierce smile curled his lips when he met her eyes, and she laughed. This was just too good. It got better every time. How could the best she'd ever had keep getting *better?* Each of his strokes hit just the right spot, which had her writhing on the sheets. His hands slid down to grip her hips, lifting her higher into his thrusts, rubbing his pelvis over her clit.

Her legs flexed against his shoulders as she worked to take him deeper, harder. God, yes. The angle was perfect, and the speed guaranteed to drive her over the edge. She was going to come. Soon. Shivers wracked her body, pleasure radiating through her until it overwhelmed her senses.

"I'm going to come," he groaned, pistoning in and out of her pussy.

Just him saying the words was enough to send her flying. Her body bowed, a high, thin scream breaking loose. Her fingers fisted in the pillow, and her pussy contracted on his cock.

"Celia!" His rough shout only spurred her on, made it hotter for her. He shuddered between her thighs, collapsing on top of her. She held him close, her body going limp with pleasure. They lay that way for a long time, twined together, their breathing ragged gasps, their pulses slowing. It was perfect.

If only it could stay like this forever.

Chapter Five

"Are we shaving your head again?" Celia ran her hand down Mason's short hair, which had grown out from the stubble in the weeks they'd been sleeping together.

Instead of showing up at closing time, he'd made an appointment, which meant he had her full attention and she'd have a harder time escaping him to run off and have dinner elsewhere. She'd been getting better at it. Telling him about her past had scared her. She'd let him too close, and this fantasy had gone too far. It was time to bow out of this little game before she got hurt.

"What do you think?" He met her gaze in the mirror, and she could see the turbulent emotions he was trying to keep in check. He knew she was backing away. He was too astute not to have gotten the memo. "Should I go back to bald?"

Danger fluttered inside her that he asked her opinion. It wasn't unusual for people to consult with their stylist, but he never had in the past. She didn't like that he'd change himself for her. "I like you with a little bit of hair."

"Gives you something to hold onto?" He pitched his voice low enough that no one could hear him over the hair dryers.

"You don't have enough hair for that yet," she whispered. If he had, she would have yanked it just then. She wasn't ashamed of her sex life, but she wasn't about to discuss it in her place of business.

A smile formed on his lips, but didn't quite reach his eyes. "Give me time. I'll get there."

Ignoring the multiple meanings and undertones that ran

through those few sentences, she swirled a cape around his broad shoulders and fastened it in the back. Grabbing an electric clipper, she shaved down the edges of his hair and trimmed around his ears.

"Come over to my house after you're done." He raised his voice to be heard over the salon equipment. "Let me cook for you this time, instead of just bringing you take out."

The thought of seeing where he lived, sharing his space with him, sent a thrill through her. To say she was curious didn't even begin to cover it. She'd turned down the offer before, and she'd do so again. It was too intimate. "No."

He tensed beneath her hands, but she refused to look up and meet his gaze. She kept her attention on finishing what little needed to be done to his hair. The sooner she was done, the sooner he'd leave.

"Oh, go on, honey. You'll have fun." Jerry gave her a sassy smile from the next station over, then ducked away and hustled for the backroom when she glared at him.

Mason ignored the other man and spoke to Celia. "You're scared."

"What?" She shut off the clipper and set it aside, dusting the stray hairs off the back of his neck.

"What was it you said? 'No one keeps me—everyone leaves.' And that's why you don't do relationships." His brows lowered. "You're afraid to plan for the future."

Shaking her head, she pulled the cape off his shoulders. "I plan all the time. I have a business, you know. Having a plan gets the bills paid."

"I'm not talking professionally, I'm talking personally." He crossed his arms over his chest, which made his biceps bulge. "You like to live in the moment, you said. That's because you're scared to think about the future. Losing your mom and your aunt, divorcing two men—those things have taught you to fear

194

what might happen tomorrow. So, you don't even dare to contemplate it. You're terrified to commit to anything that might hurt you in the end, so you live in the moment."

Every word hammered at her soul, freezing her from the inside out. She felt as if he'd stripped her bare, exposing all her most painful wounds. Tears gathered in her eyes, and shame sluiced through her that she could be so exposed with so many people nearby to witness it, though no one seemed to be paying attention to them. She wanted to curl into a little ball or have the ground open up and swallow her. She forced a scornful noise from her throat. "You just have it all worked out, don't you? You know me so well."

"I've had a year to observe you, Celia. So, yes, I do know you at least a little." His gaze in the mirror was steady, and sympathetic, but no less implacable for its sympathy. "The last few weeks have given me even more insight."

"Please leave," she choked out.

"I don't want to leave you, Celia. I want you to believe that. There's nothing to be scared of with me."

Her laugh was a grating sound. She couldn't even begin to internalize that. If there was one lesson life had taught her, and taught her well, it was that *everyone left*. They may not want to, but they did. In the end, she was going to end up alone, so she'd learned to embrace that, had made it a part of how she operated from day to day. The future was not a safe thing. The future couldn't be counted on. Maybe that made her scared, as cowardly as he made it sound, and maybe it just made her realistic.

"Your hair's done." She tilted her head toward the door. "Good-bye."

He made a frustrated gesture. "You didn't even hear a word I said, did you?"

"I heard everything you said, but apparently you haven't

been listening to me for the last year. I don't want to date you. I don't want a relationship, and you don't have to worry about leaving me because we aren't together." She folded her arms protectively over her stomach and stepped out of his arms' reach.

"This isn't finished, Celia." He planted himself in front of her, but kept his voice low so that no one who might be paying attention could overhear. "How I felt about you scared me so bad, it took me a year to face it. I get that this isn't easy. I get that it's terrifying. I don't get how you can keep running when you know how good we are together. Hasn't this meant anything to you? Or is this how *just sex* is with all your men?"

No, it was nothing like what she'd had with other men, not even her husbands, and she'd been married to them for years. But she couldn't say that out loud, couldn't bear what it meant. Mason's expression was a mixture of determination, desperation, and pain. It was the pain that stabbed at her. She should never have let this go so far that either of them was hurting. This was her fault, and it took everything in her not to sob at the tangled knot of emotions in her chest.

Mrs. Chambers burst into the salon, the bell jangling wildly as the door slammed open. Her eyes were wide and wild. "Someone broke into your apartment, Celia!"

"What?" That brought reality rushing in to slap her in the face.

She tore past the old woman and around the corner of the building. Glass littered the stairs from the broken window panel in her front door.

"Oh, my God." Her shoes crunched in the glass as she moved up the steps.

"Wait, Celia." Mason's voice rang out, a harsh command that stopped her in her tracks. "Don't go in there. I've called the police—Price should be here soon."

She stared at the shattered door, her fingers balled at her sides. Helpless anger flooded her system. Spinning around, she stomped back down the stairs and plopped down on the cement curb. She stuck her head between her knees. "Jesus Christ."

"It's a terrible thing, dear. I'm sure the police will get everything sorted out." A light hand patted her back.

This day was unreal. How had it spun out of control on every level so fast? Her stomach heaved and she wanted to vomit.

Mason sat beside her. She could feel the heat and strength of his body, and she *hated* herself for feeling comforted by his presence. He didn't touch her, and for that she was grateful. She clenched her shaking hands, and swallowed the bile that rose in her throat.

A car came screeching to a halt in front of her building, and he stirred beside her. "My brother's here."

"Okay." She sniffled as she sat up.

"Do you need help standing?" His voice was too kind to take offense that he thought her helpless.

Instead of answering, she rose slowly. People had come spilling out of the businesses nearby to see what the commotion was about. Mason went to greet his brother, and she focused on them rather than her shattered front door. Both men were big, dark haired, green-eyed, and had an air of command that made the crowd part before them. Price drew his weapon and went up the steps alone, but came back down after a few minutes.

He motioned her forward and she met him at the foot of the stairs, Mason, Jerry and Tori gathering with them. "No one's been inside since the robbery, is that correct?"

Mason shook his head. "Not since we came outside. I kept Celia away, and I didn't see anyone else try to go up."

"All right, good. I'm going to have Celia come up and look around to see if anything is missing." He met her gaze to make sure she understood he was serious. "It's best if you don't touch anything, is that clear?"

"Very." She swayed a little on her feet as the surreal experience hit her again.

Mason cupped her elbow, holding her steady as he helped her up the staircase. She felt Price following close behind them, and she girded herself for what she might see when she got inside her place.

"I know it's a mess, but do you see anything obvious missing?" Price's deep voice seemed to boom too loud behind her as she crossed the threshold.

She pulled away from Mason and looked around, taking in her tossed things. The sense of violation was overpowering. Someone had broken in and touched her belongings. Her hands shook so she stuffed them in her pockets. She tried to focus, but her mind spun. "I...I...um..."

Mason set his palm between her shoulder blades. It was so hot, it burned her skin. She felt cold, chilled to the bone. A shudder passed through her. He slid his hand up until he squeezed the back of her neck, massaging her stiff muscles. "It's going to be all right, sweetheart. Just look around, see if anything is gone. Maybe anything that might be valuable."

She swallowed, leaning into him even though she knew she shouldn't. Right now, she needed someone to be strong because she didn't think she could be. She was freezing, and he offered warmth. Pulling in a slow breath, she swept the room with a glance. "Nothing is missing that I can tell. But my jewelry is in the bedroom."

"Let's look in there, then, because I don't see anything gone either." Mason urged her forward, slipping his arm down her back and around her waist, supporting her as they walked.

Her kitchen was untouched, as was her bathroom. Her bedroom was another matter. All her things were strewn across the floor—sheets, blankets and pillows, her dresser drawers were open, the contents spilling out. She drew in two slow breaths, and Mason held her tighter. Walking to the dresser, she knelt and sifted through the rubble. "My jewelry is here. All of it, I think. At least the stuff that would be worth anything. Nothing's gone."

"Nothing?" Price squatted beside her and Mason dropped down on her other side.

Frowning, she shook her head. "I don't see anything missing anywhere. I don't even see anything broken. It's out on the floor, but it's not broken or stolen."

"Huh." Price scowled, tapping a little notepad against his thigh. "It's possible the robbery was interrupted. A noise startled him or...hell, I don't know. Why wouldn't he snatch the jewelry if he had it in his hand to throw it on the floor?"

Mason rubbed a hand down his face. "Why be careful enough to avoid breaking anything?"

"Hell if I know." The older man looked baffled.

"So...we have breaking and entering, but no robbery." Mason voiced the phrase slowly, as if that would make it make more sense.

It didn't. So, Celia asked the obvious question. "But why?"

He shook his head. "I have no idea."

"Do you have any enemies...anyone who'd be interested in scaring you?" Price's cynical gaze drilled into her, not accusing, but not assuming she was innocent either. "An unhappy customer or employee, maybe an ex you had a bad breakup with?"

She shrugged helplessly, even more upset than before. Her ears buzzed, and the strangeness of it all just made her shake harder. "No...no one. My ex-husbands are long gone, and the divorces were amicable. The salon is in good order financially. My employees and customers are happy. All my stylists were at the salon with me anyway."

"She's right, we were all there. And we're all happy little campers." Jerry poked his head in the door. He grinned at Price. "Don't worry, gorgeous. I didn't touch anything when I came back here. I didn't disturb any of the evidence."

Price rolled his eyes, but then returned his attention to the debris. Celia rose to her feet and wandered back out into the living room, taking in the chaos again. She was right. Nothing was broken. Overturned, littering the ground, but easily put back into place. It didn't make any sense at all. Who would break in, but not take anything? Who would want to break into her apartment in the first place? There really wasn't much to steal—she didn't keep anything particularly valuable. Her money was in her business, in her bank accounts.

Mrs. Chambers stood in the doorway to the apartment, and she blinked owlishly at the mess, her age-spotted hands twisting the strap on her purse. "Oh, you simply can't stay here tonight, dear. There's glass from the window everywhere. Things are all over the place."

"You can stay with Aubrey and me, of course." Flipping his notebook closed, Price stepped out of the bedroom.

Mason followed on the older man's heels. "No, she's staying with me."

"Not if she doesn't want to, brother." Price's gaze was hard, his expression unyielding.

Crossing his arms, Mason didn't back down. "She doesn't want to spend the night listening to the newlyweds thump the headboard against the wall."

Celia winced, a very clear picture of what he'd described forming in her mind. Her friend would be quieter than that for the sake of a houseguest, but that wouldn't keep them from doing the horizontal cha-cha all night. Great for Aubrey, not so much for Celia.

Her other option was Mason.

A groan spilled out of her throat. Logic told her to spend the night down the hall from the midnight mambo, lying there awake, *not* picturing her best friend getting it on, and *not* worrying about who might have broken into her place. It was the smarter choice, especially after what she'd told Mason downstairs. Spending the night at his house would only encourage him. But the last thing she could handle was spending the night alone. Her thoughts swimming, she didn't even know which way was up anymore. Wasn't that always the case with him? She shook her head at her own stupidity. "I'll stay with Mason."

"Oh, good." Tori sighed. For a split second, Celia would swear that Jerry and the elderly lady shared a conspiratorial look, a tiny smile creasing his cheeks. His expression smoothed into sympathetic lines when he noticed her gaze upon them. Suspicion fluttered at the back of her mind. They wouldn't go so far as to vandalize her house, would they? The basement thing to get her to spend time with Mason was annoying, but harmless. This? This was a violation of her home. And for what? To get her over to Mason's house?

No. She shook her head. That was insane. The strain of the day was messing with her mind.

"All right." Relief echoed in Mason's voice, but he swung into action. "Let's get some of your clothes together and head back to my place. Price and his officers can finish up here."

The older Delacroix nodded. "You'll need to file a police report, but we can do that in the morning."

"Okay." She sucked in a breath. "Okay."

They pulled up to a neat little ranch style house. A stone chimney dominated one side of the front and a wide front porch took up the other half. She hadn't known what to expect, but this wasn't it. Mason coasted into the garage and hit the button to close the door. Grabbing her bag from the back, she followed him into the house. An enormous kitchen opened into a living room and she could see a hallway with several doors leading off of it. The rooms were appointed with cozy-looking furniture. She set her things on the kitchen island and did a small spin to take everything in. "It's clean, and, you know, tidy."

Mason grinned and dropped his keys on the counter. "You were expecting mid-30's bachelor pad? Chrome and glass? Dirty dishes everywhere?"

"Well...you are a bachelor in your mid-30s." She arched an eyebrow, and smiled. It was the first one she'd managed in hours, and her face felt stiff.

"True enough." He shrugged. "I like things clean. And comfortable. Do you like it?"

"It doesn't matter what I like or not. It's your house, not mine." She was too tired to dance around the issue. Maybe coming here had been a mistake. "Thank you for letting me stay, but I haven't—"

His hand curled under her chin, forcing her to hold his gaze. "You know, I didn't invite you here to pressure you into anything. Not sex, not a relationship. Not anything."

"No relationship pressure? You promise?" Because she might just crumble and start crying if he pushed too hard. This day had been awful.

Stroking her cheekbone with his thumb, he shook his head. Tenderness bled into regret in his expression. "No. I've never meant to hurt you or scare you. Just the opposite."

"I know." She closed her eyes, her lips quivering, her heart aching. "I just don't think that I'm the woman you think I am. Despite my track record, I'm *not* the marrying kind. I'm never going to be. You deserve someone who'll give you what you want."

And that someone wasn't her. She hated having to admit it, but she couldn't avoid the truth.

Tangling his fingers in her hair, he kissed her forehead. "Now's not the time for that discussion. Let's just have some dinner and relax."

Her brow furrowed and she shook her head. "I'm really not that hungry."

"I know, but you should eat something anyway. Even if it's a small meal." He stepped away from her, and she missed his warmth.

Sighing, she managed a tiny smile. "Cookies?"

He snorted and wagged a finger at her. "Something with a little nutritional value."

The lightness of the exchange made her grin widen, and she spread her hands. "Cookies have flour and eggs and milk."

"I'll bring you some cookies with a sandwich and soup."

She wrinkled her nose at him, but didn't protest. He pulled out a stool for her at the kitchen island, and she sat down to watch him serve her.

Moving efficiently around the kitchen, he pulled a couple of cans of soup out of a cabinet and emptied them into bowls. While those heated in the microwave, he gathered the makings of sandwiches. Ham and cheese were topped by lettuce, onions and juicy slices of tomatoes. The smell of the soup and the sight of those thick sandwiches made her stomach rumble. "Guess I'm hungrier than I thought."

He grinned, brought her the soup and sandwich, and nodded toward the living room. "Let watch some TV while we eat. If you're a good girl and finish all your dinner, you can have some cookies."

She arched an eyebrow. "Chocolate chip?"

"As a matter of fact, yes." He led the way, glancing back to wink at her. "Aubrey sent them home with me. There are definite perks to having her as a sister-in-law."

"I know—she's been my best friend for three years or so." She sat beside him on the couch, setting the food on the coffee table.

It was comfortable to be there with him, eating dinner and watching a mindless television program. It was comfortable, and she didn't want it to be. She pushed the thought away, too tired by the events of the day to dwell on what she couldn't control. So, she just relaxed and went with it. What else could she do? It seemed to be her excuse for everything lately. She ignored that thought too. Add it to the list of things to beat herself up over later.

He put his arm around her shoulder and pulled her close. "How're you feeling?"

"Better." She sighed, leaning against him. "Thank you."

"No problem. You've fed me plenty of times. It seemed only fair to return the favor."

She snorted, poking his ribs. "You still owe me cookies."

He chuckled and slapped a hand over hers. "Coming right up."

"That's what I'm talking about. Sugar coma, here I come." As if to emphasize the point, she yawned. The day had taken its toll, and she was exhausted.

The smile slid off his face, and his expression fell into serious lines. "Before it gets too late and this becomes an awkward conversation, I want to talk about sleeping arrangements."

"Okay." She tilted her head, wondering what had caused the sudden shift in mood. "You're going to put me in the spare bedroom?"

He winced. "Only if you really want to. I'd rather have you

in my bed, even if we don't have sex."

"Okay." She sighed. "I don't think I'm up for sex."

"That's fine." He rose and snagged her bag from where she'd set it on the island, heading down the hall with it. "I'll put this on my dresser then. Back in a sec."

Instead of waiting, she followed him. She couldn't help it. She wanted to see his bedroom. Curiosity got the better of her. A king sized bed dominated one wall, covered in a navy blue bedspread. A television sat on a small table across from the bed, a long dresser sat in the center of another wall and a sliding glass door that opened onto the back patio took up most of the final wall.

He almost stood at attention while he waited for her to finish inspecting his space. "Well?"

She made a big show of looking around with a confused expression. It was too much fun to yank his chain. "There are no mirrors on the ceiling, no stripper pole. Not even a disco ball. This is really disappointing. What kind of hardcore bachelor are you?"

He chuckled and relaxed. "I have a surround sound system throughout the whole house and two big screen plasma TVs."

"To watch porn?"

"Sure, if you want to." He shrugged, his eyes glinting with laughter. "I usually go for ball games, but I'm open."

"Ha." She walked forward and pushed her hand against the mattress to test it. "No waterbed?"

He rubbed a finger across the bridge of his nose. "My reputation has been blown out of proportion, apparently."

"I like it. I like your whole house. It's nice." She probably shouldn't admit it, but since she couldn't give him what he really wanted, it seemed such a petty thing to hold back.

Another yawn threatened to crack her jaw, and he

rummaged through her bag until he came up with her nightgown. It was probably the least sexy thing she owned, and she'd brought it on purpose to remind herself that intercourse was not on the agenda for their little sleepover. He handed it to her and pointed to an open door. "The bathroom is through there if you want to use it."

That he didn't even push her to change in front of him, made no moves toward her, almost broke her. How he knew her well enough to understand when to push and when to back off, she didn't know. Tonight she needed comfort, and that was exactly what he was offering her. No strings attached.

It was the sweetest thing any man had ever done for her.

When they curled together in bed, an Oregon State game playing on the TV, she laid her cheek on his chest and closed her eyes to savor the moment. It was the last time she'd ever sleep in his arms. She couldn't allow it to happen again. What he'd said in the salon kept playing back in her mind on a loop. If she let this continue, it was only going to hurt him. She'd meant what she'd said—she wasn't the marrying kind. She couldn't do a serious relationship again. She wished she could, but some wounds never healed. Some fears could never be overcome. If she gave in to what he wanted, one way or another, he would leave her.

And unlike all the other people who'd gone before him, his leaving would shatter her into a million unrecognizable pieces. Because she loved him. She'd loved every single minute with him, and she *wanted* to give him everything. If she did so, and the inevitable end came, she would never, ever recover.

Those fairy tale dreams starring him as her Prince Charming disintegrated, and she finally stopped wishing they could come true. Even if he was a knight in shining armor, she was nobody's princess. It was unfair to them both to keep pretending otherwise.

Chapter Six

It had been four days since she'd left his house. The stiff, painful look on his face when she'd gone still haunted her. Even worse was the empathy that shone in his gaze. He'd kissed her forehead and let her go. He hadn't pushed, hadn't demanded.

It had almost broken her. Almost.

Only the knowledge that it would hurt so much worse in the long run if she stayed had kept her feet moving and had kept her away for days. Since then it had felt like she was just going through the motions. She opened the shop, she worked, she occasionally met Aubrey for coffee, who worried and pointed out she looked pale. Like that helped.

She made sure she was the first one in the salon and the last one out every day, and today was no exception. It was easier than lying in a bed that she'd never share with Mason again.

"Hey, is Mason okay?" Jerry rolled in for the day, yawning and stretching, a smile on his face as if he'd had a long, gratifying night.

Now, there was a mental image she didn't need. And his obvious satisfaction did nothing to lighten her mood, especially since he'd been one of the people to push her toward Mason in the first place. She managed to keep the irritation out of her voice, barely. "How should I know? I haven't seen him in a couple of days."

His face fell into distressed lines. "But what about the accident? I thought since you were here that meant he was doing better."

The blood froze in her veins. "What do you mean? What accident?"

They stared at each other for a moment, an eternity.

"Jerry, *what accident?*"

His Adam's apple bobbed as he swallowed. His gaze went behind her and the bell over the door jingled. "Delacroix."

She spun, expecting to see Mason, but instead Price stood there. His face was drawn and haggard, his emerald eyes so like Mason's. She swayed, her knees went weak and all the blood fled her face. What hit her the most wasn't that Price reminded her of Mason, it was that she'd never seen an emotion like that on his normally world-weary and cynical expression.

He looked scared.

"Morning, Celia."

Celia wiped her cold, clammy palms on her pants. "Jerry said there's been an accident with Mason. What happened?"

"How did he know—" Price shook his head. "Never mind. Can I speak to you privately for a moment?"

The bottom dropped out of her stomach. There was no other way to describe the hollowed, gut twisting downward rush of dread. She knew this feeling, this moment of utter terror and helplessness. She'd felt this the day her aunt called to let her know she was dying.

"Um. Sure. The supply room in the back?"

"Sounds good." He nodded toward the back of the shop.

Her legs shook so badly, she didn't know how they stayed under her for the short walk. Price shut the door behind them, and stood there silent for a long, unbearable moment. She couldn't take it, and her worst fear burst out. "Just tell me...is he dead?"

"No." But the uncertainty in his voice said more about Mason's condition that anything else could have. "He was at a

Make Me Believe

house fire and part of the building collapsed on him. His arm is messed up, and he suffered from smoke inhalation before they got him out."

"How bad?" She reached out, latching onto his wrist.

"They aren't sure yet. They're running some tests." He swallowed, his voice growing hoarse. "He looked pretty fucking pale and out of it when I saw him."

Her hand tightened on his arm. "Thank you for telling me."

"I'm here to take you to him. He'd want you there."

She wanted to argue that, say she didn't mean enough to him for him to need her, but she didn't. The truth was, she wanted to be there. She didn't want to stay here and pretend everything was okay while she slowly went out of her mind with worry. She wanted to be there the *second* they had news.

"Let me get my purse." Since Jerry had foisted her off onto Mason so many times, she would let him deal with rescheduling her clients for the day.

It served him right.

"Mason?" The barest whisper slipped past her raw throat. It felt as though she had been screaming, but she'd swear she'd kept the pain inside.

He looked ashen, with mottled bruises marring his skin. His arm was swathed in bandages, and she could see blood had seeped through the white cloth. This hospital was just as she remembered from Grace's time here. Cold, ugly green tile on the floor. Harsh fluorescent lights and an antiseptic smell that stung her nose. She wrapped her arms around her waist, trying to hold herself together. If she relaxed for even a second, she feared she might crumble.

One of his eyes opened, the other was so bruised it was swollen shut. "Hey, honey."

His voice was weak and raspy, but he tried to smile at her, and it was all she could do not to sob.

"Hey." The word cracked in the middle, and she held herself tighter.

"I've been thinking about you."

She swallowed. "You've had time for that?"

"Yep." He held out his good hand, and she moved forward to take it.

She tried not to hold on too tight, didn't want to hurt him. "Oh."

Swiping his tongue over cracked lips, he held her gaze. His green eyes were bloodshot and red-rimmed. "This had to scare you pretty bad. I'm sorry."

"I don't have any right to..." She shook her head. "I left you."

Saying those words were a blow to the chest. Without meaning to, she had done to him exactly what she hadn't wanted him to do to her. Agony twisted inside her, ripping at all the emotions she'd been suppressing since she'd met him...since her mother had died. It had been so long, she didn't even know who she'd be without it.

His chuckle was a painful thing to hear, and he squeezed her fingers. "I understood why. I knew you'd come back."

"How could you know that?" She hadn't even known it herself. Until she'd seen him again, she'd thought she could walk away clean. That eventually the pain would fade the way it had with Grace and her mother. Someday, she'd be okay again. Someday, she wouldn't wake up with the loss fresh in her mind. The difference was, Mason hadn't died. Mason was still alive and right in front of her, if she just had the courage to reach out and take what he'd offered freely, and that she'd rejected, wholly and harshly.

He'd been right. She was scared. Terrified to move forward after her divorces, so certain that every man would give her more of the same. Afraid of the future, so she'd ignored the possibility of a future with any man who might have been interested. Only Mason hadn't given up after she'd refused to give in.

No wonder she loved him. He'd believed in her even when she was too scared to believe in herself.

"How could I know? Because I've been there. I told you. This wasn't easy for me either. But with something this good? You have to face your fears." The corner of his mouth quirked in a grin. "I knew you would."

"You did?" Hot moisture welled in her eyes.

"Yeah." He swallowed hard, his smile falling away. "I understand if my job makes things...harder for you. Today had to bring back some of what you went through with your aunt and mom."

"It did." She nodded. She couldn't lie to him, especially considering that one of his fiancées had run from their relationship because of the kind of thing that had happened today. His job was dangerous. It came with risks. But she already knew that it wouldn't hurt any less for him to die when they weren't together—today had demonstrated the stark truth of that. Love was the thing that changed the equation, not just being together in a relationship. "But this isn't like them. This reminded me that I was letting myself lose you *before* you'd died. They left me alone, but not by choice. *I* left you alone willingly. That's worse."

Lifting her hand to his lips, he kissed her. "This could happen again, you know."

"And you could die. I'm aware of that. I could get run over crossing the street too." She shrugged, blinking back the tears. "I told you I like to enjoy the moment, so...maybe we can keep doing that. Together."

It was the scariest thing she'd ever said, admitting that she wanted to plan some kind of future with him. Even something as small as that, she'd sworn she'd never do again, but today had shown her that she couldn't walk away.

The offer fell far short of what he probably wanted from her, and her insides quaked, waiting for him to react, to say something, to give her some kind of response.

"I love you."

The statement was bald, as forceful and straightforward as the man himself. His green gaze was open, told her how sincere he was. He loved her. Period. End of story. She burst in tears, burying her face in her free hand as sobs wracked her. It was too much. It was everything. It was perfect, and she didn't know how to deal with something so good being given to her.

He kissed her fingers again, then her palm and the inside of her wrist. Pulling her down, he pressed her forehead to his. He waited until her breathing calmed and the tears slowed. "You said I deserved someone who could give me what I want."

"Yes." Her voice was waterlogged, so she nodded for emphasis.

His lips brushed hers, his hand tangling in her hair. "What I want is you, and you're the only one who can give me that."

"I love you, Mason."

A smile curved his mouth. She could feel it against her lips. His gaze lit with something beyond joy. "I know."

"You *know?*" She pulled back a bit, her eyebrows arching.

He chortled, and it quickly turned to a coughing fit. "Oh, damn. Don't make me laugh." He stopped hacking after a minute and sighed. "I knew you loved me, sweetheart, I just didn't know if you'd ever admit it."

"Well, I did." She pursed her lips and made a face at him.

Curling his hand around her jaw, he stroked his thumb over her lower lip. "I don't need you to believe in marriage or happily-ever-afters or any of that other fairy tale bullshit that tells you what you're supposed to want. I just need you to believe in me, believe that I'll stick it out with you no matter what, and I'll never leave you of my own free will. Start there, and I think we'll be doing pretty good."

Tears burned the back of her eyes again. "I'll try. For you."

Chapter Seven

"So, I've been thinking..."

"Yeah?" She bent over the bathroom sink, rinsed the cleanser off her face and dried her hands on a towel. "About what?"

Mason's voice rumbled from her bedroom. "This whole engagement and marriage thing hasn't gone very well for us in the past."

"Understatement, but yes." A laugh bubbled out of her as she ran a brush through her hair, then set it on the vanity.

It had been a month since the fire, and Mason had gone back to work two days before. He was on light duty for another couple of weeks because of the arm, but he'd come straight to her place when he'd left the firehouse. He sat naked in her bed, propped against the headboard. His long legs were crossed at the ankle, and he watched her leave the bathroom and walk toward him. "Damn. You are so beautiful."

"Thanks." She did a little pirouette in the vintage, lacy chemise. "Do you like it?"

"Is that even a question? I love it." He grinned. "I have every intention of enabling this obsession you have with fancy lingerie."

Her eyebrows arched, and she smiled back at him. It felt good. She'd been happier in the last month than she had been in years. Maybe forever. It was still hard to trust it, but it got a little easier every day. "Oh, yeah?"

"Yeah." His gaze blazed pure fire when he looked at her,

then he shook his head and chuckled. "You're distracting me."

She winked. "You're welcome."

Rolling his eyes, he sobered. "So, what I was saying...I really don't have any desire to be engaged again, just like you don't want to be married again."

"Right." She froze at the end of the bed, suddenly wary that this fragile sense of safety she'd developed in the last few weeks was going to get rocked. "I'm with you so far."

He crossed his arms, his muscled chest rippling with the movement, and the pink skin of the new scar on his arm shining bright against his flesh. She forced herself to look away from it, to meet his gaze when he spoke. "So here's my proposal... I'd like to *not* be married to you for the rest of our lives."

Now there was an interesting thought. If they were never engaged, never married, they could never get divorced. Considering the ugliness both of them associated with matrimony, she had no desire to ever associate marriage with Mason. What she had with him was so much better than that. "And would this be an exclusive non-marriage?"

"Fuck, yeah." His dark brows snapped together in a scowl. "I'm not sharing."

She hummed in her throat. "Would this non-marriage include a white picket fence and two-point-five kids?"

Shifting on the bed, he uncrossed his ankles and sat forward. "I'm open to kids, but I'm not a fan of white picket fences. But, hey, if you really want one, I can put one up around my front yard."

"No, thanks." She shuddered. "I have nightmares about white picket fences."

"Whatever you want." His gaze locked on her face, the intensity of his expression telling her how much the wrong answer would hurt him. "So...what do you say?"

She drifted a little closer, brushing a hand up his calf. "Would it work for you if I said, *I do*?"

"Yeah." He grinned, a surprised laugh cracking out. "I do too."

The moment stretched on forever, more honest and beautiful than either of her wedding ceremonies. This commitment was one she hoped would last forever. She wanted it, and she'd work her ass off to keep it. More importantly, she knew he would too. Mason held on to the things he wanted with both hands. No one understood how persistent he was as much as she did.

He patted the mattress beside his hip. "Come here."

"Are you sure you're up for anything?" A dart of worry passed through her, and her gaze fell to his wounded arm.

"After a month of having you in my bed, but not getting to have sex with you? I'm more than *up*." His rising erection certainly proved his point.

She snorted, though her body heated at the evidence of his arousal, and the need to cement their vows to each other in the most carnal way possible. "You know what I mean."

"The doctor cleared me to go back to the firehouse, and before you ask, yes, I asked if sex was okay. It is." He gave her an impious grin and folded his hands behind his head. "But if you're worried, I'll just lie back and let you do most of the work."

"You've been waiting a whole month to use that line, haven't you?"

"Yep. You know me so well."

She did, actually. It amazed her how well she understood him after so short an amount of time, but there it was.

"I want you." He reached for her, and when she put her hand in his, he tugged her into his lap. She straddled his thighs, her negligee riding up until there was nothing between their sexes. The position alone sent excitement winging through her, and her core went slick with juices.

The head of his cock slid over the lips of her pussy as he leaned forward to kiss her. It was just as good as the first time. Sweet and hot and irresistible. She pushed her tongue into his mouth, craving the taste of him. Waiting all these weeks to have her hands on him again was more than she could bear. His palms stroking down her back, heating the silk of the gown, was heaven. Her nipples tightened, thrusting against the soft lace that made up the bodice of her chemise. The stimulation made her shudder.

He bit her bottom lip lightly, and she whimpered into his mouth. She rocked her body against his, loving the friction, the slide of her softer curves against his hardness. It was addictive, the way he made her feel. He kissed her chin, her jaw, and she let her head fall back when he moved to her neck. His lips were soft, and then he used his teeth. A moan spilled out of her, and she jerked at the sharp contrast. He licked and sucked at her neck until she felt lightheaded with the rush of need. Of its own accord, her body undulated, pressing her sex to his, retreating, only to return.

Groaning, his hands bracketed her hips, pulling her down to grind against her clit. She cried out, her damp core flooding with more moisture. It was too much. She reached behind her and guided his cock to her opening. He shoved upward while she pushed down, seating her on his cock. The fullness of his penetration was almost painful after a month of celibacy. Almost.

"God, Mason. I love the feel of you inside me."

His chuckle was a rusty sound. "I love being inside you. I just love you, period."

The sweetness of those words made her sex clench tight. It left her reeling, gasping as he shoved his cock deeper into her

217

pussy. Her fingers curled around his shoulders, her eyes meeting his...and she saw his every emotion shining there, just for her. Love. It was more than she'd ever thought she'd have again.

A sob caught in her throat, a quiver running through her. One corner of his mouth kicked up in a smile, and empathy shone in those green eyes, so clear and beautiful she wanted to cry. He got where she was coming from, why she had doubts, and he waited for her to be ready. He understood, perhaps more than any other person she'd ever met in her life.

"I love you," she whispered.

His eyes sparkled the way they did every time she said those three words, and his little smile blazed brighter. He took her hand and placed it over his heart, where she could feel it hammering in his chest. "That's all I'll ever need. You are my heart and soul, baby."

A tear slipped down her cheek. He reached up to brush it away with his thumb, and she turned her head to kiss his hand. "I love you so much."

She said it again because she had to, because she couldn't hold it back, not from him. This feeling had been building for so long, she didn't even know when it had started. Perhaps, like him, she had known it from the beginning and been too scared to face it. That this one man was perfect for her, the sum of all her fears, and that she'd have to let go of those fears if she wanted to keep him.

Cupping the nape of her neck, he drew her down for a kiss. The movement made his rigid cock shift inside her, and she moaned, her body reminding her forcibly that her cravings were yet to be satisfied. She could feel the grin on his lips as they played over hers.

He broke away. "Move on me, Celia."

There was no way to refuse, and she didn't want to. She

didn't want to refuse him anything. Arching her hips, she drove her pelvis against his, angling herself so his strokes had the best effect. It was electric, gave everything a deeper meaning. It was no longer just sex, but a physical expression of all the things she'd locked inside for so long. Things she could now say.

Had it ever been *just sex* with him? She laughed, the sound tripping over a moan as he pushed her harder, faster, his hands sliding over her sweat-slicked flesh. She lifted and lowered herself on his cock, the heat and friction enough to drive her crazy. And she loved it.

Ecstasy gathered deep within, streaked over her skin, rising in an unstoppable riptide that dragged her under. She let herself go, released all control, and gave in to him, to herself, to her heart. Orgasm seized her inner muscles, milking the length of his cock. Still she rode him, rocking herself on his dick, letting her climax continue as her sex pulsed around his thick shaft. She never wanted this to end, this perfect moment with him.

His gaze locked with hers, letting her see everything he was feeling. His face flushed with lust, and love reflected in his eyes. She could see how he struggled to keep from coming, how he tried to fight the end of this, just as she did.

"Come for me, Mason. Come inside me."

The sound he made was like a human volcano erupting. His hands clamped over her hips, jerking her down to the base of his cock, forcing himself as deep as he could go. His come jetted into her, filled her. He shuddered underneath her. "I love you, Celia. I love you so fucking much. I'll love you forever."

She believed him.

Epilogue

Tori propped her shoulder against one of the big oaks in the town square. Celia and Mason sat having coffee with Price and Aubrey outside of Bean There, Done That. Tori didn't worry about them noticing her. Even if they did, they wouldn't recognize her. Gone was the disguise she'd been sporting for the year she'd been in Cedarville. No more old lady for her, she was back to her normal self, and they would see a young woman with long, dark hair that rippled to her waist. She ran her hand through it, glad to be rid of the bun on her head. Guardian angels could look like anyone they wanted, and she'd been in that disguise far longer than she'd anticipated.

"This was a real bitch of an assignment." Jericho echoed her thought as he stepped up beside her and rested one palm on her shoulder.

"And you had to hook up Price and Aubrey before you became a gay stylist, *Jerry*. Cedarville rode you hard and put you away wet."

"Don't call me Jerry." A shudder ran through his big form. Just as she did, he looked like himself again. No longer slender and effeminate, he was tall, muscular, and had a face too craggy to be called pretty. "Price and Aubrey were tough nuts to crack, yeah. Celia was worse, I think."

"Mason too." She shook her head. "I was starting to fear he'd never pull his head far enough out of his ass to realize he was in love."

She'd also worried that Celia wouldn't be able to move forward into a permanent relationship. Then again, who was she to judge? She'd had to learn the same lesson herself. Accept the harsh truths of the past and believe in the possibilities of the future. It had taken Jericho's persistence to get the message through to her. For an angel who specialized in pushing soul mates together, it was sad she'd needed the reminder, but there it was.

"Job well done, my love." He slid his hand up to cup the nape of her neck.

"You too." She slanted him a glance. "Though I have to say, mentioning the guardian angel thing in that note to Mason and Celia was a little over the top."

He snorted. "Says the woman who vandalized Celia's house."

Tossing her hands in the air, she arched her eyebrows. "You *wanted* me to do something drastic."

"So I did." He grinned at her, and her heart flipped. "We did good."

"Yeah, we did." She was damn proud too. There were times when she'd had more than a few doubts that even some help from her angelic *woo-woo* wasn't going to get Celia and Mason together. "Where do you think the Powers That Be will send us next?"

Jericho's broad shoulder dipped in a shrug. "No clue, but I hope we get some down time before our next assignment. I know what I'd do with a little time off."

"What would you do?"

"You." The smile he gave her was hot and wicked and utterly unangelic.

Heat flooded her body, just as it always had whenever he looked at her like that. She'd known the man for over a hundred years, and he still did it for her.

"Let's go, my Vitoria." He held out his hand, an invitation, a promise.

She twined her fingers with his, no hesitation. It had been a long, winding road getting here, but she believed she'd found what she needed, and she'd helped a few lost soul mates get what they needed too. It felt good. A grin tugged at her lips, and she turned with Jericho to walk toward their future. Together.

Their work here was done.

About the Author

Crystal Jordan began writing romance after she finished graduate school and needed something to fill the hours that used to be eaten away by homework. Currently, she serves as a librarian at a university in California, but has lived and worked all over the United States. She writes paranormal, futuristic and erotic romance.

To learn more about Crystal please visit www.crystaljordan.com. Send an email to Crystal at crystal@crystaljordan.com or join her Yahoo! group to join in the fun with other readers as well as Crystal: http://groups.yahoo.com/group/crystal-jordan.

It's all about the story...

Romance

HORROR

www.samhainpublishing.com

CPSIA information can be obtained at www.ICGtesting.com
Printed in the USA
LVOW070827140513

333702LV00004B/326/P